To The Dogs

BOOKS BY NICOLE MCINNES

100 Days
Brianna on the Brink
The Jilliad
A Flash Fiction Christmas (Editor)
Freedom Flash (Editor)

To the
DOGS

31 VERY SHORT STORIES
ABOUT MAN'S BEST FRIEND

Edited by Nicole McInnes

Altitude Press

Contents

SCIENCE FICTION

MYSTERY, SUSPENSE, SPOOKY & PARANORMAL

Introduction

In late 2023, Altitude Press put out a call for submissions for a dog-themed flash fiction anthology to be released in the fall of 2024. Having published similar projects previously, we thought we knew what to expect—namely, a modest number of solid offerings from unknown or emerging authors.

We weren't prepared for the stream of fantastic stories that were soon bombarding our inbox on a weekly (and sometimes daily) basis. As founder and editor-in-chief of the small press, it was my job to consider submissions not only in terms of individual quality but also in terms of how well each would fit in with the overall anthology concept.

Over time, a harmonious grouping of themes concerning humanity's canine companions developed into a cohesive whole, despite the broad spectrum of genres and categories represented: literary fiction; speculative fiction (which is often used interchangeably with science fiction and fantasy but which, in this case, mainly means experimental in craft); science fiction; mystery (combined with suspense, spooky, and paranormal); and myth (combined with folklore and allegory).

The stories you'll read here were written by over thirty different authors from all over the world, and it is to those authors I wish to express my deepest gratitude. Without their words, this anthology would not have been possible. It is my sincere hope that you, Dear Reader, will derive as much enjoyment and inspiration from these tales as we have gained in presenting them to you.

~Nicole McInnes

LITERARY
FICTION

Carlos and the Flamingos

BY VALERIE HUNTER

ON TUESDAY MORNING, LINDA discovers a riot of pink across the street, a flamboyance of plastic flamingos planted in her neighbor's front yard. She saw the flyer at the library last week and knows it's some sort of fundraiser: a certain amount of money paid to pepper someone's yard with a dozen flamingos, a certain amount paid by the recipient to have them removed and sent on to someone else's yard. Linda finds the whole thing ridiculous; if anyone dared to pollute her yard in such a manner, she'd uproot the trashy birds herself and give the organizer a piece of her mind to boot. Not to mention hold them responsible for fixing all the little divots that would doubtless be left behind, marring her pristine grass.

Carlos, however, is entranced. Linda's dog has always been strange in both appearance and personality. He's a mutt through and through, with a lab's ropy tail and goofy smile, a shepherd's alert ears, and a hound's sad eyes and sonorous bark. He's a good size—Linda can't abide little dogs, forever yipping and nipping—but he frequently forgets that. He's always attempting to cower in spaces too small for his body, such as under the dining room chairs, behind Linda's desk, and in the little nook next to the bookcase.

Carlos has no interest in typical dog things like squirrels, cats, and mailmen, but he enjoys barking at pumpkins and garden gnomes, is deeply distrustful of footballs, goes crazy at the merest whiff of coffee, and is compelled to relieve himself on every dandelion he sees.

Linda stopped trying to figure him out long ago and just accepts him for who he is. Everyone has their peculiarities, after all, and Carlos's are easy enough to live with. She adopted him from the shelter six months after her husband's death because a dog seemed like just the right amount of company, of responsibility. He came to her with his personality already intact and his name already given. It's a ridiculous name for a dog, but she never considered changing it. The name belonged to him; it would be cruel to take it away.

Carlos sits by the window all morning and barks himself into a frenzy at the sight of this flamingo army until Linda finally draws the curtains to get some peace.

Later, when she takes him out, he insists on crossing the street but refuses to get too close, slinking past with eyes only for those bright birds, a low growl in the back of his throat.

"Now, now," Linda says, hurrying him on. She knows the growl is a bluff, knows he's secretly terrified.

They make it through the rest of the walk without incident and without running into anyone, for which Linda is grateful. She doesn't consider herself unfriendly, but she also doesn't really see the point in inane small talk. Fortunately, Carlos is similarly inclined; he'll give other dogs a cursory sniff and a wag, but then he'll keep going. Linda will say, "See you later," over her shoulder to the dog's owner, a tinge of an apology in her voice, but she's secretly delighted that Carlos never lingers.

Unfortunately, he seems to find the flamingos worth lingering over. With each trip outside, he grows bolder, moves closer, pauses longer in front of the tacky birds. He is obsessed, consumed, clearly more than a little in love with them. He wags, struts, swaggers past, begging the flamingos to notice him.

One morning, they step outside to find that the wind has tipped three of the birds beak-first into the dirt. At the sight of them, Carlos gives his most melancholy bark, then looks up at Linda with a pleading expression.

"Not my job," she tells him firmly.

He sits and continues to stare at her. He is seven years old, but he can still employ puppy-dog eyes when he needs to.

"They're not real." She feels silly whenever she tries to reason with Carlos, but that doesn't stop her from doing it.

He lets out a plaintive whine.

Linda knows from experience that she can stare him down if necessary. Instead, she sighs and looks around. Once she's sure no one's watching, she reaches over and rights the flamingos.

Carlos grins his approval, tongue lolling.

"Lovely, aren't they?" someone calls.

Linda flinches, then turns to see one of the down-the-street neighbors approaching with her French bulldog. Linda knows the dog's name—Cindy Lou—but not the neighbor's.

"So bright and cheerful," the neighbor goes on as Cindy Lou and Carlos waggle and sniff. Linda forces herself to smile and make some vaguely agreeable noises, because what else is there to do?

"We're having a barbecue next weekend," the neighbor says. "I'd love it if you—"

Mercifully, Carlos untangles himself from Cindy Lou and sets off at a trot. "We'll talk later," Linda calls. "Bye!"

"Bye, Linda!"

Carlos looks over his shoulder a few times, as though to ensure Cindy Lou isn't making any kind of mischief with the flamingos, and they continue on.

That night in bed, Linda wracks her brain trying to remember the neighbor's name, but it doesn't come to her. In her defense, this woman moved in during the waning days of Greg's illness, when Linda could barely remember her *own* name. Afterward, the woman dropped off a casserole as well as a condolence card. Linda knows she still has that card bundled away with all the others in an old shoebox in the back of the coat closet, but she can never quite bring herself to dig it out.

She turns her restless mind back to the flamingos. What does Carlos see in them? Do they remind him of something in his previous life, before he was Linda's? She ends up dreaming about a dozen Carloses, each riding an enormous, live flamingo. They fly away—a garish, pink flock—and Linda is all alone. She wakes up feeling silly but also strangely hollow. She googles whether flamingos can fly and is amazed to find they can.

The plastic flamingos have an extended stay. Maybe it's a status symbol, the recipient flaunting that he's worthy enough to be punked. Linda has never exchanged more than a hello with this particular neighbor, but judging by his flashy car, trendy clothes, and weekly landscaping service, he's all about appearances. Eventually, he'll pay to have the birds sent elsewhere. She has an urge to warn Carlos, but, of course, she can't.

With each passing day, Linda dreads the birds' inevitable disappearance more. For a moment, she even considers asking the neighbor to pass the flamingos onto her next, but that would never do. There are limits to what she can put up with, even for Carlos. Besides, it would only be delaying his pain. Eventually, the birds have to go.

Sure enough, after ten days, the flamingos disappear as suddenly as they arrived. Linda notices at breakfast and postpones Carlos's walk, but that only works for so long.

When they finally exit the house, Carlos's shock is palpable as he all but stumbles across the street. Linda has to drag him past the neighbor's yard and keep him from trespassing and sniffing every inch, as though he might be able to find the flamingos if he just tries hard enough. When they return home, he spends the rest of the day by the window, clearly hoping the birds will reappear in a puff of magic.

Every walk thereafter, he insists on sitting in front of the neighbor's yard for a moment of silent mourning before he gets on with his business. Linda finds it horribly embarrassing, but she stands beside him, respecting his grief.

At the supermarket the following day, Linda spots three flamingo lawn ornaments lying in a heap with twenty-five percent off stickers on their wings. They're slightly smaller than the ones on the neighbor's lawn, their eyes a little beadier, but Linda still stops to consider them. She can buy one. She can buy all three. Put them in the backyard where no one will have to see them except Carlos.

But what if he doesn't like them? What if he resents this pathetic attempt to replace the glorious flock? So she doesn't get them, and goes home feeling she made the right choice.

Carlos is depressed all week. Linda does what she can for him—extra treats, extra attention, extra walks—but there's no use trying to cure loss.

A few weeks later, when Carlos is beginning to act a bit more like himself, they have the misfortune to encounter another flamingoed yard on a different street. Linda watches as Carlos stares in shock then keeps going, nose in the air, tail limp, pointedly ignoring those terrible birds who abandoned him.

She knows it's all for show and that, inside, his heart is breaking. She feels tears well in her own eyes, and, for the first time in years, she allows herself to cry.

Valerie Hunter teaches high school English and has an MFA in writing for children and young adults from Vermont College of Fine

Arts. Her stories have appeared in publications including Beneath Ceaseless Skies, Capsule Stories, OFIC, *and* Sonder, *as well as multiple anthologies.*

The Dog of My Childhood

BY VICTOR SOOTHO

THE FEAR RETURNED TO me before I became aware of it. It had been years since I was home. As I passed by the Johnsons' compound on my way to an important appointment, a familiar feeling emanated from deep in my history. I hurried my steps, as I often did in my childhood. I thought about running, but then thought better of it. I passed the fence without much ceremony, paused, and looked back.

I hadn't thought of the Johnsons or their dog, Red, in all my years of being away. Why should I? Those were childish memories, and one is rightly expected to forget childish things past a certain age. But my mind still remembered to be cautious. The fear was still there. It was, however, faint, more like a residual fear than anything serious.

Looking back and not seeing Red gave me a new sort of anxiety. His raucous barks would've been a welcomed homecoming. Everything was quiet, and maybe Ol' Red was the victim of the quietness also. It was evening; the children should've been out to play.

I felt momentarily guilty when I realized the stillness was partly my fault. My wife and I had left this place, after all. We hadn't given our old home new children to break the silence and interact with dogs like Red.

The memories returned as I stood there: I remembered running back and forth in front of the Johnsons' compound when doing errands which required me to pass by. Red was always in an anticipatory mood by the fence, barking and hopping to and fro whenever he caught a whiff of me. I would examine whether the gate was securely closed each time while tentatively increasing my stride. Then, when I was face-to-face with the little red devil, I'd take off.

Red would run with me along the length of the fence, but I'd keep going even beyond the corner post, imagining there was a hole he'd discovered and that he was following me. I would keep running until the barking grew fainter and eventually stopped. On my way home, I'd often find Red still waiting by the end of the fence as if anticipating my return. The old familiar dance would resume: I'd escape once more, and Red would sound one last triumphant bark at keeping the intruder away.

For me and my friends, teasing Red was always a reliable pastime. During this time, we would revel in our cowardice or put on a countenance of bravery, depending on the mood of the day.

A favorite game was, of course, seeing who could get closest to the hostile Red. If one of us was feeling especially reckless, we'd shove the adventurer forward. Red would pull back at this unexpected lunge, and the shovee would unleash fury on the shover while the rest of us laughed. To diffuse the situation, an imaginary crown of victory would be placed on his head. If no clear winner emerged for the day, there would be debates and recollections about who got closest and who scared Red the most while the dog watched us from afar. To make our cases, each of us would describe Red's breath, his general odor, and how his eyes looked. We'd repeat these games until Red tired, or we tired, or until the setting sun forced us to return home for the night.

We only locked horns once, me and Red, but to this day, that moment still remains the main source of my fear. It was an uneventful afternoon when we boys walked past the Johnson's and suddenly someone screamed, "The gate is open!"

Red's fur glowed bright orange; he was like a canine fireball hurtling towards us. Attempting to grab a stone as I ran, I stumbled. My friends had scattered, but when they realized they were out of harm's way (due to me now being the sole victim), they stopped to watch the drama unfold.

I was on my knees in the dirt. I thought of many different possibilities—rabies and being limbless, for starters. As Red bared his teeth, he emitted a predatory vibration. I turned my body to face him as he went back and forth in a semicircle around me. I had twisted my hand back so that he couldn't see the stone I was holding. Surely, the antagonizing my friends and I had done over the years was enough motivation for him to attack. I felt guilty and even more fearful as I understood the years of frustration he was about to unleash on me—perhaps rightfully so.

But then something shifted. In an instant, I realized that the reason he was circling me was to see what was in my hand. His expression was more curious than hostile. After a while, I showed him the stone. Red looked at it and then at me. It was then that I understood the nature of our relationship and tossed the stone. Red quickly pounced and went after it. He inspected the object, barking almost gleefully. Then, he licked it and went back home.

I stood there for a few minutes as the memories washed over me, but Red didn't come out. Growing impatient, I approached the Johnsons' unlocked gate. Red was resting on his stomach near the house. He looked up, saw me, and uttered a single, pitiable bark. After standing up with great effort, he plodded toward me. He stopped a few feet away, though. Was it recognition, or maybe resignation that I wasn't afraid, and the faint barking was his last resort?

I heard a door screech open and then close with a clatter. From the corner emerged Eli Johnson.

"Who goes there?" he asked.

"It's me," I said with a wave. "Michael. Jeannie's boy."

He squinted and smiled in recognition. "Ah, Mikey," he said. "So, you've come back to see us."

"Only for a while. Red has grown old."

He sat on a worn stool by the wall and motioned for me to sit, too. "Yes," he acknowledged. "All of us have, but not as bad as him. Dog years and all of that." He paused for a moment and continued. "If Red was any other dog, I suppose I wouldn't have kept him. But he was always gentle."

I smiled. "I remember the one time he got out. I thought he was going to maul me. It turned out he just wanted to play."

"Yes, he was more like a burglar alarm," Eli said, slapping his knee as he leaned back in laughter.

Red watched us as we talked for a while about the past.

"He used to make our afternoons interesting. Back then, we were only wasting time. I didn't realize those wasted hours were some of the best parts of my life."

The old man nodded. "I think he would say the same if he could speak. He used to sleep all day anticipating the moment you boys would return from school. The afternoon sun was his alarm. He would be restless the entire day until he saw the first uniformed body." I looked down at the resting Red. A fly happened by his nose, and he only lazily shook his head. Even this seemed to be a great effort.

I was late for my appointment. I felt guilty leaving, like I was abandoning an old friend in his time of need. I knew that, after getting the documents I came for, it would be impossible to find the free time to come back. What would I even be coming back to, really? I hadn't thought much about Red in the years I'd been away. Would I have earned the right to mourn him? After the hundreds of hours we'd spent testing each other, this impromptu half-hour visit didn't do him justice. I felt guilty that this place, which had once been my everything, could now feel so foreign and that paperwork could be distracting enough to make me forget everything.

As soon as I stood to leave, Red perked up. He tentatively approached me.

I hung my head, then reached out and slowly scratched him. "You be a good boy now, alright?"

He only growled by way of an answer.

It felt strange, this routine, to call him a 'good boy' when he was older than me in dog years. It felt strange when I ruffled his coarse, aged fur. The only thing that had remained distinctly him as I'd remembered from years ago were his eyes. They hadn't lost their sharpness, and I hoped they recognized me.

As Red stared at me like he did so many years ago, I became certain that there was recognition. There was no animosity. They were those same eyes which had looked at me when I'd thought he was going to maul me. Those eyes which had comforted me and told me that we were friends.

When Red realized the scratching session was over, he went back to his spot and rested once more. I told him I would return soon, and I meant it.

I meant it when I said it then.

Victor Sootho is a writer from Maseru, Lesotho. His writings draw inspiration from his history and personal life.

Honey

BY MARIE ANDERSON

A CHRISTMAS TREE BLINKS in the front window of the house across the street from ours. I think it's not a real tree. We put a real tree in our front window. Their tree is too violently green, too implausibly, perfectly shapely. A Victoria's Secret model of a tree.

At night, since the day after Thanksgiving, the blinking, electric bulbs on the tree in the house across the street from ours spasm greens and blues, on and off. I sit in our parlor in the dark, looking out the window at that blinking tree, while my husband watches sports on his big screen in the den. I don't understand sports. I don't watch TV anymore unless my husband is around to turn it on and find a movie for me. Too many gadgets to press to make the TV listen to me, too many buttons on the gadgets with just arrows and numbers that don't make sense.

So, I watch the neighbor's tree. The lights on that tree shiver on and off like drunk, demented fireflies. I used to chase fireflies when I was a little girl. I'd catch a few and put them in a jar so they could blink just for me. I always let them out of the jar before I went to bed. Real firefly lights are soft and sweet. Not like those Christmas tree lights in the house across the street. I'm glad my husband and I are not prone to seizures. Blinking lights can trigger seizures. Our cat was prone to seizures. Taco. Sick as he became, he always used his litter box, never left his solids or fluids where they didn't belong.

He's buried in the yard of our old house in the city.

We are cat people, but my husband says we're done with pets.

My husband hates dogs. He was bitten in the face when he was eight years old. A scar still etches his left cheek.

When people hear his scar story, they ask why he'd put his face so close to a dog.

A daughter brought home a puppy once. Her best friend had let her pick the puppy out from the litter that was living in their basement. The daughter cried when my husband said no. I'd already named the puppy. Frisky, I named her, because she never stopped moving, except when she licked my face and my daughters' faces, and that made us all laugh, and I didn't even get mad when she peed on the couch.

But my husband said no.

So, Frisky went back to the litter living in the basement. I wonder where she is now.

I don't hate dogs, but now I'm afraid of them. In our old neighborhood in the city, I wasn't afraid. This past summer, we downsized to a little brick ranch in a suburb with curvy, confusing streets. I didn't want to move. I knew where everything was in my city neighborhood where we'd lived for 35 years and raised some daughters. My husband and my daughters said the city wasn't good for me anymore. They said that if I was going to get lost on my daily walks, it was better to get lost in a quiet, safe suburb. I don't know what the hell they mean. I never got lost in my old city neighborhood.

My husband complains there are too many dogs in our new neighborhood.

On my daily walks, I veer into the street to escape a dog's barks and lunges and its owner's assurances that their doggie is perfectly safe and friendly. Once, when I veered into the street to escape a dog and a tall, bearded man filling the sidewalk, a car almost hit me. It slammed on its brakes, honked its horn, and, from the back seat, a wolf barked.

On garbage mornings, I see her, the lady of the house across the street from ours. We are each dragging bags of trash and recyclables to our respective curbs. She pretends not to see me until I call out, "Good Morning!"

She grudges out "morning" back, leaving out the "good."

We don't know each other's names, though we've been living here since summer, and now it's winter, and we—my husband and I, her husband and she—are all wrinkled and graying and the same religion. I know this because I avoid her line at Sunday Mass. She's a Eucharistic minister, and her husband, hunched in the front pew, beams at her while she flips the Body of Christ into cupped palms.

Her husband sits in the front handicapped pew where there are no kneelers but lots of space for his walker. I think he has Parkinson's, like my dad did, because his hands quiver.

My husband doesn't go to Mass. He sleeps in, drinks freshly-ground Columbian coffee, and reads two fresh Sunday newspapers unwrinkled by me, while I sit in a pew praying for salvation for our faraway children. None of whom this past Thanksgiving took time away from their busy lives to do more than Skype us with their spouses and their children, whose names I sometimes can't remember. "Hello, chickens," is how I greeted them on Skype.

One of the chickens asked, "What year is it, Grandma?"

They all giggled when I replied, "The year of living dangerously."

And then another one asked, "Who's the President, Grandma?"

"Who cares?" I replied, and someone scolded, "Quit the teasing, kids."

"But she's used blue crayon on her eyebrows again, Mom!"

"How's Frisky doing?" I asked the daughter.

"Who's Frisky?" one of the chickens clucked.

"Who's Frisky, Mom?" the daughter asked.

"Frisky! She licked our faces! Remember how that tickled? How we all laughed?"

"Mom! That dog we had for a day? That was over thirty years ago!"

"Grandma, how come your eyebrows are blue?" a chicken asked, and all the chickens laughed.

Taco never tested me with questions or laughed at my eyebrows. I miss him so much. My sweet boy. His favorite food was chickens. I couldn't find my brow liner, so I used a crayon.

Right now, knitting on my couch facing the front picture window, I watch her, the lady of the house across the street from ours, not pick up the dog shit her bouncy golden retriever deposits in the snow on our front lawn.

I fling on my coat, run outside.

She and the dog—not leashed!—are already half a block away.

I slip, fall onto my snowy front lawn, try to get up, manage to turn myself over. I'm on my back, flailing my arms, my legs. Why can't I get up? I close my eyes to stop the tears.

Something soft and wet snuffles my cheek.

I open my eyes and see the lady and her dog. She pulls the dog away from me.

"You're making a snow angel! How fun! Sorry about Honey. She ran away from me to investigate."

I lift my arm. "Help me up?"

She smiles, hauls me up.

"Thank you," I say.

"No problem," she says. "I live across the street. I'm Irene."

"Ramona," I say. "Nice to meet you." I look down at the deposit the dog left earlier on my snowy lawn.

"I'm so sorry about that," Irene says, pointing at the poop.

"I usually have poop bags in my coat pocket, but—"

"No problem," I interrupt. "Shit happens."

She laughs, and then I laugh, too.

Honey barks. I reach down and pet her.

"Hi, Honey," I say. Honey licks my hand. I smile. "Frisky likes to lick my face."

"Oh? You have a dog, too?"

I shake my head. "We're cat people, but we're done with pets."

Honey licks my hand again.

"Honey likes you," the lady says.

"Your Christmas tree," I say to the lady. "It crazy blinks."

She looks at her house across the street. I look, too. No tree fills the window, just the back of a sofa.

"Oh," I say. "I guess you took it down."

She laughs. "Thank God Christmas is over. I can't wait for summer sun and nighttime fireflies! Well, it was good to finally meet you, Ramona."

"Yes, good." I say. What the hell is her name?

The dog. The dog is Honey. "Well, it was good to meet your Honey," I say.

Whew. She smiles. "Honey's my ice breaker. Everyone loves her."

"Your husband," I say. "He has Parkinson's."

She stares at me. Then nods. "Would you like to come over sometime? Meet him? Visit?"

"My dad had Parkinson's," I say. "And my family thinks I've got a little bit of not remembering things."

She nods again. "Sucks."

"But I remember most things," I say.

"We all have something breaking," she says, "if we live long enough."

"Sucks," I say.

We both laugh. Honey barks and nuzzles my leg. And I remember. The lady's name is Irene.

"Me too, Irene," I say.

She looks at me, her eyes squinching, her brows pinching. "Sorry?"

"Me too," I repeat. "I can't wait for summer sun and nighttime fireflies. I bet Honey likes to chase them."

The lady smiles. "She does."

Marie Anderson is a Chicago-area, married mother of three millennials. Her stories have appeared in dozens of publications, most recently in Calliope Interactive, Shotgun Honey, After Dinner Conversation, Mersey Review, Third Wednesday, *and* Fiction on the Web. *Since 2009, she has led and learned from a writing critique group at a public library in La Grange, IL.*

Rex's Wake

BY HARDING MCFADDEN

THE NIGHT OF THE day they buried Rex, the family had a wake for him, though none saw it coming before it arrived. Earlier in the day, around the hill in the backyard where they'd planted his mortal remains, the lot of them—Mom and Dad, Junior and Betty, and their new pup, Stu—had all stopped to cry over the loss of such a good dog. The kids had hung onto Mom's dress, and Dad still had dirt up to his elbows from digging the hole and filling it in with remains and memories and soil. All the while, Stu had sat there, a look of confusion on his young, uncomprehending dog's face.

Rex had been with them for more than a decade, so when he crossed over it was the end of an era. He'd been along for the ride with Mom and Dad longer than either of the kids, and he had more miles under his padded feet than a good car. In the end, he was mostly blind, mostly deaf, and far less willing to take long walks with the folks than he'd been as a pup. But right up *until* the end, he'd been a good boy, even when you had to pick him up to snuggle, since he couldn't jump up anymore.

He'd died right after church, lying in Dad's lap while the old man cried like a baby. Mom, Junior, and Betty had been around him, in no better shape than Dad, and they'd all petted him as he left. For a few minutes after Rex stopped breathing, his heart stopped beating, and his mostly blind eyes finally unfocussed, they stayed where they were, knowing that when they let him go, they'd be letting him go for the last time. The idea of that was every bit as painful as him having died in the first place.

Inside of twenty minutes, Dad rolled up his sleeves and got the shovel and pickaxe to dig the hole while Mom and the kids wrapped him up in his favorite blanket and packed away some of his things in an old shoe box that they'd labeled with his name, month of birth, and date of death. Under all of these factual words, they'd written a solid truth:

A Good Dog

The lookout from the hill where they buried him was a sight to behold; it was one of the reasons they'd bought the house in the first place. A gradual slope leading down to a gently flowing creek thirty yards away, the hill had a dozen lively trees that shed their leaves every autumn to blanket the earth before the onset of winter. In the summer, they provided blissful shade, endless perches, and limbs to hang from. In the distance, some miles away, was the town, sleepy and old-fashioned and beautiful. It was a pleasant view, regardless of season, and one the family felt was appropriate for Rex's last resting place.

Needless to say, the rest of the afternoon was a melancholy affair. When they were hungry, they ate. When the stress of the day got to them, they rested. Each met their misery privately as they reached out a wanting hand to have it met by nothing but air filled with ghosts and fresh, painful memories.

Stu trolled around the house for hours looking for his friend. It was simply that Rex had always been there playing, or yelping, or growling when he'd wanted nothing more than for the younger, much more energetic dog to just leave him alone. That he was gone now was a concept so alien to the pup that he couldn't grasp it. Stu was certain Rex was just hiding from him, or missing, and that if he looked hard enough and long enough, he'd find his buddy and they'd play again.

When the sun was finally setting, and the family had had about as much of the day as they were able to stand, they all got ready for bed, said their prayers and their morose goodnights, and went their separate ways.

It was near midnight when Stu woke Dad by scratching at his sleeping hand, begging to be let out. Grumbling, Dad stood up from bed and trudged through the house to open the kitchen door for the insistent pup. He sat on the back porch to wait for Stu to finish his business.

The moon was nearly full that night. It washed away the stars—all but the brightest ones—and bathed the earth in a silver glow. There was the slightest of breezes. In the distance, the town was asleep; only two streetlights were lit, and every window was dark and empty. Inside the house, the rest of the family slept a much-needed sleep. It all felt empty, and lifeless, and sad.

When Stu started his baying out there in the silvered darkness, it pulled Dad back from insubstantiality to the world at hand. Shaking his fogged head, he stood and walked out into the yard and down the hill, his bare feet creating small, green waves as they moved through the grass.

"Where are you?" he asked the night, moving toward the sounds of the dog.

The baying was filled with sadness and longing, devotion and fear. It was mournful and confused. Pitiful. All day long, Stu had been searching the house for his friend but hadn't found him. And now here he was, out in this eternal night, calling for Rex to come home.

Dad found Stu sitting next to the mound on the hill where he'd buried Rex hours earlier. The pup sat there with his head thrown back, begging the world to return his friend to the pack. Each howl was like a shard of pain tearing its way into Dad's heart. Slowly, he sat next to Stu and petted his back while looking out into the night.

Meanwhile, having been awakened by the noise, Mom, Junior, and Betty appeared and sat near them in silence, feeling the weight of the loss with them. Within arm's reach was the mound, the place where, earlier that day, they'd planted the shell of the dog but not the dog himself. They paid little mind to that pile of dirt. Instead, they looked up into the sky at the brilliant moon and the few bright stars whose light reached out to them.

Nobody expected Dad to start baying along with Stu. Even he hadn't figured on doing it until the bizarre sounds escaped him.

Within a few heartbeats, the others joined in, belting out their own pain and sadness, releasing the feelings of loss and rage. They were letting go—not looking for their lost friend but saying a farewell to him. Letting the night, and the world, and the universe know that he'd been a good dog. That he'd gone off to somewhere better now, and it was alright.

In the distance, one at a time and very slowly, as the slight breeze carried their goodbyes along, light began to flicker on in the town—window lights, then porch lights—like a spreading flame, a pyre to light Rex's passing.

In time, the howling died down, and the lights flickered off again as the town went back to sleep. Mom and Dad helped Junior and Betty back to bed after each had scrubbed the grass and dirt from the bottoms of their feet and the seats of their pajama pants.

Stu stood out there for a few more minutes before coming inside to lay in his bed and mourn in silence.

~for Casey, a Good Dog

Harding McFadden is a Pennsylvania-based writer who works primarily in the New Pulp world. His work has been printed in magazines and anthologies, most recently in the publications of Airship 27. He has published two novels (The Children's War *and* The Great First Impressions Trip), *a pair of short story collections* (The Judas Hymn *and* Making Monsters), *and a collection of essays and articles* (Opinion as Fact).

Daisy

BY JULIETTE BEAUCHAMP

GRACE STOOD ON THE cold concrete floor of a rural animal shelter and covered her ears against a cacophony of barking. There were dogs of every size and color in the row of cages, each desperate for a moment of her attention. They pressed their snuffling noses against the chain link doors and scrabbled frantic paws at the gap below.

She walked slowly, overwhelmed, stopping when she reached the very last cage in which huddled a small dog of indeterminate breed. There was hound blood in there, evident by the droopy ears and the tricolored coat, but the dog's nose was narrow and her body long and slender.

Hound mixed with collie, or maybe spaniel. This dog was silent, chocolate eyes rolling at the surrounding din. Grace noted the cage number.

Back in the reception area, she leaned against the desk as the smell of bleach burned her nose. The barking was lessened by the cinderblock walls, but it was still loud enough to make her head hurt. There was a poster on the wall with a cartoon dog gazing up at a cartoon man. The dog's eyes were red hearts, and the caption read: *I Want to Be the Person My Dog Thinks I Am.*

"See anything you like?" The woman behind the desk wore bright blue eyeshadow and a faded scrub top covered in cartoon characters. A pinned nametag read "Carol."

"Yes. I think so. Kennel twelve...a hound mix, maybe?"

"Oh, that's Daisy. Yeah, poor little thing, she's not doing too well. Misses her family."

"You mean she's not a stray?"

"Nope. She was turned over. Her owners got a new puppy and..." Carole shrugged casually, as if this was a common story.

Grace realized it probably was. "Who does that?"

"Honey, you'd be shocked. Wanna take her for a walk?"

Grace nodded, and Carole passed her a slip leash. "Go right on out the back, you'll see a little path. You'll have to come back through the front door though. The other one will lock behind you."

"Thank you." Grace took the leash and went back to the kennel area. "Hey girl." She opened the kennel door and held out her hand. "Wanna go for a walk?"

Daisy gave her hand a polite sniff and stood quietly while Grace slipped the leash over her head. It was warm outside; late May sunshine filtered through oak leaves as they ambled along the dirt path. Daisy paused to inspect a bush, and Grace looked around. Beside them squatted a low-slung building constructed of the same cream-colored cinderblock as the kennel. A sign over the door read: *Crematorium - Staff ONLY.*

Daisy moved on from the bush, blissfully unaware of the nearby structure. A few minutes later, they reached the end of the little path and went back inside.

Carole glanced up from the computer. "Whaddya think?"

"Has she had many people interested in her?"

"Daisy? Nope. Most people want something younger. She's already ten."

Grace looked down at the funny little dog. Daisy gazed serenely back at her and thumped her tail, once. "And um, how much longer does she have here? Before...you know."

"Let me check her file." Carole clacked a few keys. "One more week. We'll try to transfer her to another facility at that point. But if everyone else is full then...you know."

"I'll have to think about it. I'm getting ready to move." Grace saw Carole's eyes narrow slightly and hurried to add, "But if no one else takes her, please call me?"

Carole jotted down the phone number and pinned it to a corkboard beside her computer as Grace led Daisy back into her kennel. The dog's tail was once again clamped tightly between her legs, but she offered no resistance when Grace lifted her back into her cage.

"Good girl." Grace patted her and left, pushing through the back door so she wouldn't have to see Carole's disappointed expression again.

"Did you adopt one?" It was raining at home, and her mother's voice was crackly over the old landline.

"No, but there is one I like." Grace plucked at a loose thread on her sweater.

"So why didn't you get it?"

"I don't know, Mom. Is it the right time? I'm about to move, and I have so much to do before then…I don't even know why I went to the shelter."

"A young woman living alone should have a dog. Does your new apartment allow pets?"

"Yeah, it does." Grace had checked the lease paperwork.

"Then go back and get it!"

"But do I really *need* her? It's a big responsibility." Grace didn't mention that, sometimes, she struggled to even leave her apartment, weighed down by the crushing loneliness resulting from a recent breakup. She had initiated the separation, hurt by the man's continual disparagement of her body, yet she still felt abandoned. Was it fair to bring a dog into that?

"I don't think you're looking at this the right way."

Grace rolled her eyes to the ceiling. "How so?"

"You may not need the dog, but maybe it needs you."

Daisy took a few dainty steps through the front door and looked around the apartment's living room, which was empty except for a plush new dog bed and a pile of taped boxes. Her tail thumped as she sniffed around.

"Ground rules. No using the bathroom inside. And don't chew up my shoes, please." Grace patted the little dog's head and passed her a biscuit. "Other than that, I'm pretty easy to live with."

They fell into a routine. Walks at seven, twelve, and five. Breakfast immediately after the first walk, and dinner immediately before the last. Biscuits whenever Daisy asked, which she quickly learned to do every few minutes (until the first vet visit, when the nurse frowned at the scale and recited a host of ailments overweight dogs could develop).

"Sorry, girl." Grace rubbed Daisy's floppy ears. "I need to lose a few pounds myself. We'll do it together." The biscuits were swapped for green beans and a long, meandering walk was thrown in on weekends.

Neither of them lost any weight, but they did enjoy exploring the new town, strolling down alleys, and discovering hidden gardens. Grace felt emboldened and freer than she ever had, like having a dog to walk gave her a right to take up more space.

On one of those walks, they met Sam. He soon became a regular presence in the new apartment. Daisy would sit politely next to his chair during dinner, and Grace would pretend she didn't see the occasional tidbit passed between them. At night, Daisy would fall asleep on her dog bed but inevitably sneak into Grace's bed after the humans had drifted off, her nose touching her tail, her body forming a perfect circle in the space behind Sam's knee.

"I love you Grace," Sam said one day, not long after they became exclusive. "And you might not be ready to say it back," he continued with a mischievous grin, "but I'm pretty sure at least Daisy feels the same way about me."

When Sam proposed to Grace the following year, she accepted—with the stipulation that Daisy be the ring bearer.

"I wouldn't have it any other way, babes," he said.

The three of them drove to Grace's hometown in Alabama for the wedding. They kept it simple, an informal ceremony in her parents' backyard.

Daisy, who'd never chewed anything in the two years since Grace had brought her home, shocked everyone by pulling off her collar and tearing into the attached ring pillow (found online, dog participation in weddings being surprisingly popular), swallowing both rings along with the stuffing.

Amid shocked twitters from the few people in attendance, Sam raised his hands. "People, people, it's alright. We can still say 'I do'...it's just not official until Daisy doo doos." After the resulting groans, Sam grasped Grace's hand and smiled. "I love you, babes. But for the next couple of days, Daisy's your dog again."

Grace laughed and agreed. Two days later she donned a rubber glove and fished the rings out of a fresh pile. Daisy sat next to her, and when Grace looked over, she could have sworn the gray-muzzled little dog was laughing.

On the last day of their Alabama visit, Sam and Grace took Daisy hiking at a nearby nature reserve.

"Watch out for gators," Grace said as they stepped onto the boardwalk spanning a marshy area. "Look." She pointed as an armored snout poked through the shimmery green carpet of duckweed before receding.

"Holy smokes!" Sam had never been further south than Missouri. He picked Daisy up. "C'mon, pups. It's safer up here."

They navigated the boardwalk with no further sightings, and Sam lowered Daisy back to the ground. "That was wild. I had no idea there were such creatures in your sweet little hometown."

"Oh yes. Here be dragons...Sam, stop." Grace held up her hands. "Don't move."

Sam froze. "What? Is it a gator?" His voice was barely above a whisper as he looked down and saw the snake just inches from his right foot. "Oh my God! What do I do?"

"Back up slowly. It will leave."

But the snake, a fat cottonmouth, didn't leave. It gaped at Sam, displaying the trademark white mouth, and slithered forward.

"Nope, nope, nope!" Yelling now, Sam jumped backwards but caught his heel on the buckling lip of the boardwalk and fell heavily. His feet slipped out from under him, one heel glancing against the snake, which hissed again and struck, narrowly missing Sam's calf.

Sam cried out, and then there was a snarling and a flash of fur as Daisy rushed forward, teeth bared. The cottonmouth whirled and hissed as the little dog growled and leapt, feinting back and forth as the snake lunged again and again.

Sam struggled to his feet. "Daisy, leave it!"

Daisy turned to him, and the snake struck, fangs sinking deep into the gray muzzle, before slithering off the boardwalk and into the marsh.

"Daisy!" Grace screamed as she scooped up the dog. Daisy's heart thrummed under her hand as a thin trickle of blood ran down the dog's nose and dripped onto the ground beneath them.

"C'mon. Let's get her to the car, quickly." Sam pulled out his cell phone. "Do you know where the closest vet office is? No? I'll call your mom."

Grace's mom directed them a few miles down the road, and they careened into the parking lot on two wheels. Because Daisy's muzzle was swelling at an alarming rate, the receptionist wasted no time in taking her from Grace and rushing her into the treatment area.

"Doc! Get out here!" Grace heard her yell before the swinging door closed, and she burst into tears. "Please

let her be okay," she sobbed as she leaned
husband.

Sam stroked the thin scar on Daisy's now totally white muzzle. "Do you remember when she saved me from the snake?"

"How could I forget? Brave, sweet girl." Grace wiped her nose. "Ugh, I thought I was prepared for this day."

"I don't think you can ever be ready for something like this." Sam smiled as Daisy licked his hand. "She's on her way to a better place. I truly believe that."

"I just wish there was more we could do for her. I wish the chemo had worked." Grace's eyes flicked to the clock. The hospice vet would be arriving at any moment to do the unthinkable. "Dogs deserve to live forever."

"Babes, you rescued her from certain death four years ago. She got an extra shot at life...you were there for her when she needed you."

His phrasing struck Grace as familiar, and she thought back to the conversation she'd had with her mother after first visiting the shelter. She laughed quietly through her _ears, remembering that sad, lonely girl she'd been before Daisy. "No. It was the other way around. It was me that needed her."

Juliette Beauchamp grew up reading every-thing she could get her hands on. As an adult, she's still usually reading two or three books at a time. She lives on a small farm in Virginia where she caters to the whims of a variety of animals and tries to keep up with her toddler.

Neighbors and Dogs

BY ZARY FEKETE

A LOT MAY BE learned about people by noticing how they relate to dogs. In the neighborhood where I live in Budapest, it is possible to pass well over a hundred people on the street on any given day. In the few square blocks surrounding my flat, many of those people walk to their destinations (few of them have their own cars), and when they walk, most of them have a dog walking with them.

Two large thoroughfares cross one another here in the 11th district of Budapest. One is Bartok Bela Street, named after the famous ethnomusicologist. The other is

Bocskai Street, which takes its name from the Magyar Revolt against the Turkish Empire in the 17th century. Most streets and squares in Hungary are named after famous figures and events from Hungary's past, and it is possible to treat yourself to a history lesson just by walking a few streets in any direction.

Two triangles of smaller city streets are cut from the crossing of the two large boulevards. One triangle is nestled against the Danube River, and it is quite gentrified. It contains a modern mall and the Budapest University of Technology and Economics, one of the finest schools in the country. It has sleek restaurants and brand-name stores. It has a Starbucks. It is the Budapest the mayor of the city would like to show to the world.

The other triangle is a series of streets and avenues that have largely been frozen in time and are almost identical to how they looked a century ago. Here, in the other triangle, is my neighborhood. It's where you will find another Budapest. Less modern. Not as wealthy. Given to weedy street corners and vacant lots containing old, crumbling, socialist-era structures. You will also find mothers and fathers pushing baby carriages to the local park, following the doctor's orders to give their newborns plenty of fresh air. You will see dogwalkers bringing their dogs of varying sizes to the street corners to socialize, and it is not uncommon to see a large German shepherd licking the head of a dachshund.

Here, in this older Budapest, each city block contains most of what you need. Around the corner from my apartment is the butcher's. He gets his cuts of meat from southern Hungary, from the city of Szeged, where it is still common for families to butcher their own pigs and where a morning butchering means the family will be eating fresh pig's trotters in a rich, red stew that night. The butcher's mother is in the last stages of cancer; recently, the butcher has brought choice cuts of meat as gifts for the nurses who are treating her. He has a small poodle who lives in the back of his shop while he works. He often feeds the dog scraps that are left over from cuts of meat that have been processed throughout the day. I see him ferrying the dog home after work, tossing it bits of fatty beef or morsels of pork from a plastic shopping bag.

Across the street from the butchers are the neighborhood flower ladies, mother and daughter. They have owned their flower stand since the 1950s. If you go to buy flowers with your child, they'll give the child a fresh

Gerber daisy or a sprig of baby's breath. They live on the outskirts of Budapest and bring their lunch with them each day—usually a few slices of bread spread with lard which they eat with fresh tomatoes and peppers. The mother is ninety-three. Her daughter is seventy and un-married (*I never found my true love,* she'll say if you engage her in conversation). The flower ladies have a Vizsla, a Hungarian breed. Vizslas resemble greyhounds and need a lot of exercise every day. On the days they bring him to work, their dog sits obediently beneath the jars of flowers, but his favorite thing is when one of the ladies brings him to the neighboring park for his afternoon run.

If you walk a few streets in the other direction, you'll find the neighborhood watch repair shop. The owner is a mustachioed man in his seventies who uses a wheelchair. He has a watchmaker's magnifying glass permanently clutched in his right eye. When you talk with him, you see a face Picasso might have painted, with one regular-sized brown eye and one large eye that constantly rolls back and forth as he tells you stories about the many watches he has worked on over the years. (Once, he is proud to note, he fixed the watch of the prime minister back in the 1960s.) The watch man owns a small French bulldog who sits between the desk clocks on display. The dog's wide-set eyes have an odd resemblance to those of his owner. When I visit, I see four revolving eyes (two human, two dog) greeting me as I enter the shop.

You will also meet, if you walk down Bartok Street, an elderly man who lives in a storefront. He tells the story of his grandfather, who was the patriarch of the entire building in the 19th century. *He owned the whole block,* he'll say. At one point, the building housed a leather-repair shop. *I learned the trade from my father,* the old man will tell you. Now that he's retired, the shop has become his home. He outfitted it with a creaky cot, salvaged from the vacant lot a few streets over. The shop no longer has electricity, and if you walk by in the evenings, you'll see the old man reading by the light of a candle. During the day, he reads while sitting at the front door. There's a small flower growing out of a crack in the pavement under the front window, and he waters it every day. The old man lives by himself, except that's not quite true: In the past few months, he has adopted a mongrel puppy, a wiry creature with brown and black fur. When I asked where the dog came from, the man said he was walking home across the park one evening, and the dog approached him with a wagging tail.

When the man couldn't find any owner waiting for the puppy, he brought the dog home with him instead.

Why do so many in this neighborhood own dogs? It's not surprising. You might find a block like this in any city in the world. People crave companionship, and a dog offers it obligingly and without judgment. But perhaps I'm trying to ask a deeper question when I ask why so many of my Hungarian neighbors have dogs. To keep a dog in this European city is difficult, after all. Most apartments have only one main room. The walls are thin, allowing barks to travel easily between living spaces.

The answer, I suspect, is tied to the history of this city, this country. Here in central Europe, Hungary has changed rapidly from one historical season to the next. Today, it is a democracy with gleaming shopfronts if you know where to look. But the socialism of the 60s, 70s, and 80s has not been forgotten. Back then, the grocery stores had much less than they do now. Cigarettes came from Russia and had a harsh taste. Breakfast cereal was imported from Yugoslavia. Coca-Cola was relatively new and exotic. The most common car was the Trabant from East Germany, which ran on a mixture of oil and gas.

People made do with what they could, often sharing with neighbors who had less.

But regardless of those seasons of feast or famine, Hungarians have always loved their dogs. Today's neighborhood walk through this modern city recalls walks with canine family members from decades past. Every family remembers weedy vacations to Lake Balaton or the low mountains of northern Hungary with a Puli or Pumi at their heels. Children grew up with their parents reading the childhood novel *Bogancs* (which means *thistle*) to them. It's the story of a shepherd's lost dog whose adventures take him through a traveling circus's wagon wheels and through the clutches of thieves before he finally winds up back home again.

I think about these things when I wander through my neighborhood's streets, smiling at fellow pedestrians as they walk with their dogs. The love for four-legged companions is built into the character of this country. Even the most famous Hungarian poet, Petofi Sandor, lovingly recalled evenings with his dogs in his poetry.

Tomorrow, when I wake, it will not be from the sound of an alarm clock. It will be what wakes me most mornings—the happy sounds of dogs being walked through this neighborhood framed by the two large boulevards. I am already looking forward to greeting my neighbors and giving their dogs a friendly scratch on the head.

Zary Fekete grew up in Hungary. He is the author of the novella Words on the Page *(Dark-Winter Lit Press) and the short story collection* To Accept the Things I Cannot Change: Writing My Way Out of Addiction *(Creative Texts). You can find him on Twitter/X and Instagram @ZaryFekete.*

Janko and Sadie

BY PHIL BARNARD

SHE WAS A LITTLE black-and-gray dog that looked like nobody loved her. Most of the dogs in the neighborhood had the same look. But this one seemed to have a way about her that made a person stop and pass the time of day.

Janko stopped and bid the mutt hello. New in this country, with few to talk to, he was pleasantly rewarded when the little dog started to lick his hand. As he continued his way down the road, she followed him. And when he sat down on a park bench, she jumped up and settled in his lap.

"So, little lady, you want to be friends?"

The dog tilted her head at him and smiled.

"Good, I like that. My name is Janko. What do they call you?"

Squinting, she sniffed the air, revealing nothing.

"You must have a name. I can't just call you dog. You are pretty. I shall call you Mariska. That was my mother's name. She was very pretty, too."

When Janko got up from the bench, she jumped to the ground and looked up at him expectantly.

"You want to walk with me. Good, I got some food back in the room. But I don't know if you like Polish sausage."

She did.

At first, there wasn't always enough money for them to eat regularly. Mariska would head for the garbage cans behind the deli at these times and feed herself.

Before long, Janko got a job doing cleanup in a commercial soft pretzel bakery. New Yorkers loved the big, soft bread treat, sprinkled with small rock salt crystals. There was always a dish of salt on the counter for those who liked more.

He also went to night school, where he studied to become a citizen. The day of his oath ceremony, the whole kitchen crew, including his boss, showed up to cheer the loudest before taking him to lunch.

"Janko, congratulations," his boss said. "You are now a citizen, and you get to complain about the government like the rest of us."

"If I want to complain about the government, I go back where I come from."

After work, he loved a glass of beer. He felt at home in Clancy's, a neighborhood bar, full of people who got their hands dirty working for a living. Many of them were new arrivals, like himself.

Mariska went everywhere Janko went, including Clancy's. If it wasn't crowded, she would sit on an empty stool next to him. Otherwise, she would sit in his lap and peer over the bar rail.

One night in Clancy's, Frank called out, "What kind of name is Mariska?"

"I dunno. It was my mother's name. She was pretty like my little friend here."

"Well, it's a good name in some languages," the Hungarian sitting next to Janko said. "But in mine it sometimes means 'bitter.'"

That ain't no bitter dog," another customer chimed in. "You should call her Sadie."

"Sadie? What kind of name is that?"

"In my country, it means Princess," a nearby Irishman proclaimed.

Janko thought about this. "That's a good name. She's a princess, alright."

Pretty soon, everybody was putting in their two cents.

Frank spoke up louder than the rest. "Here, I'll show you. Hey Sadie, come here and get some lovin'."

She jumped out of Janko's lap, walked across the bar, and sat down in front of Frank, wagging her tail.

Scratching her behind the ears, Frank said, "See? She likes the name. Don't you Sadie? Janko, don't look at her. Just say, *Sadie, come here*. I bet you a beer she'll come to you."

Janko did, she did, and from then on, she was Sadie.

Life improved for them when he got a pretzel concession in the busy 86th Street subway station on the IRT line. Business was good, and they soon moved to a nicer apartment in the same neighborhood. Janko said he and Sadie were comfortable there.

She would sit on the counter and visit with the customers. The transit cops always warned Janko when the health inspector was riding the train, checking on the food vendors. At these times, Sadie would jump down and go to her kennel under the counter.

Everybody loved Sadie, and she loved everybody. Everybody except the thug that tried to mug Janko one day as he was closing up the concession. When the thug raised his hand to strike, Sadie leapt off the counter and bit his hand. He swung her left and right, but the little dog hung on as long as she could. Finally, she couldn't. She flew through the air, crashed into a nearby stone wall, and slid to the floor in a way that made Janko fear she was broken.

At the same time, a transit cop got off the train. As soon as the would-be robber was in handcuffs, the cop was on his radio, calling for help to get Sadie to the vets.

She was, indeed, broken. The vet said he could set the bones, and she should make a good recovery. It would cost about five-thousand dollars. He might as well have said a million.

That night, Janko went to bed upset and worried. He did not sleep well.

The next day, the story spread among Janko's customers and the customers at Clancy's. They all knew Janko couldn't afford a bill of that size.

When Janko emptied his tip jar that evening, there was a hundred-dollar bill, a fifty, three twenties and a lot of fives. Clancy put a jar and a sign behind the bar, and it was soon filling up.

Every day, the regulars would ask, "How's Sadie doing?" until Janko was forced to put out an official, grapevine daily report.

It took a while, but, little by little, Sadie healed. One night in Clancy's, Frank said, "You know, I think Sadie would get better a lot quicker if you took her to work. She probably misses her friends as much as they miss her."

Frank was right. Each morning Janko would carry her to work and place her in her doggie bed on the counter.

Soon after, when Sadie's special friend, Maria—a little girl in a wheelchair—came by, Sadie jumped off the counter and up into Maria's lap. Maria's mother smiled as Sadie licked the little girl's cheek, making her giggle.

Janko thought the picture very beautiful. He looked up toward the ceiling and very quietly said, "Thank you."

One day, Maria was wearing a bright, flowery head scarf. It was not tied under her chin, but rather wrapped around her head.

"That is a very beautiful scarf, Maria. Where I come from, they call it a babushka."

"That's a funny word."

"Yes, it is. A babushka is a grandma, and they wear a scarf like that. But not pretty like yours. Yours is very nice, and you are beautiful wearing it."

While Maria and Sadie were busy visiting, her mother leaned in and said, "It's for the cancer. She was very unhappy when the chemo took her hair. It was nice of you to say that."

"Well, it's true," Janko told her. "Besides, little kids shouldn't have to deal with cancer. That's not what childhood should be about. They all need love, and little girls need to be told they are beautiful, especially when they don't think so. Even from an old pretzel seller who talks funny English."

Maria's mother shook her head. "No, Janko, you're more than a pretzel seller. I see you when someone hasn't got enough for a pretzel. You give them one. Especially the homeless. You are a good person."

"Ah, I don't know about that," Janko said, waving a hand through the air. "But I don't forget when I was hungry and people—strangers—gave me something to eat. If we all helped just a little, there would be less suffering in the world."

That night at Clancy's, when he told them about the conversation with Maria, Frank said, "You're a philosopher."

Janko raised an eyebrow. "Now I know you already had your second beer."

"True, but you are still a philosopher."

"Maybe I should raise the price for my pretzels."

"Nah," Frank said, shaking his head. "You ain't *that* good a philosopher."

They both had a good laugh.

The next time Janko saw Maria's mother, he asked about children with cancer.

"The hospital where Maria gets her chemo has a whole ward filled with those kids," she told him.

"Where is this place?"

"It's Sloan-Kettering on York Avenue, between 67th and 68th Streets."

Janko thought about this for a moment. "You think they would let me and Sadie visit the kids?"

"I'm sure they would," she said. "Call them and ask."

"I will do that."

As it turned out, the hospital staff were happy to have Janko and Sadie come and visit the children. From then on, the two of them would spend their days off with the kids. Janko would tell them stories about where he came from, and Sadie would visit each child.

On Christmas Eve, he read them "The Night Before Christmas." Sadie wore a big red bow, and he had a Santa hat. He even got Frank, from Clancy's, to dress up as Santa Claus and hand out presents. Because Janko had never married or had children, these kids became his and Sadie's family.

The grayer his hair got, the slower Sadie became. He would pick her up so she could sit on the counter. She still loved to visit with the people, and her regulars always brought her treats.

One day, Janko looked up and saw a pretty young woman standing at the counter. He recognized the bright babushka she wore around her head. "Maria, is that you, all grown up?"

"Yes, Mr. Janko, it's me." When she pulled the babushka off, beautiful black hair tumbled to her shoulders.

Sadie remembered her, too. Wagging her tail, she snuggled herself against Maria's outstretched hand.

"You are well?" Janko asked her.

"Yes, no more cancer. I'm married, and we have a little girl. We named her Sadie."

"That's nice. Janko would be an awful name for a little girl."

Maria smiled. "I heard you are retiring."

"It's true," he said with a nod. "Tomorrow is our last day. I think Sadie will miss coming here. I know I will. But it is time for us to take it easy."

"The two of you helped a frightened little girl be a little less scared," Maria said. She leaned over the counter, gave him a kiss, and hugged Sadie. "Thank you, Mr. Janko." With that, she turned and disappeared into the rush-hour crowd.

Janko wiped a tear from his cheek.

Late in the fall, a friend found Janko sleeping with the gods. He was sitting in his big chair with the unmoving little dog in his lap. From the look of it all, he just passed away and Sadie followed him, like she had done so many times before.

Phil Barnard's journey has taken him from the three-piece suit world of Madison Avenue to the log rafts of Alaska, from the cockpit of an Air Force plane to driving a taxi in NYC the night JFK was assassinated, and from tending bar in a Playboy Club to owning and operating several pubs and restaurants. He lives and writes in southern Idaho.

Other People's Dogs

BY DIANA ASHMAN

I ABSOLUTELY LOVE DOGS. Truly, I do. Especially dogs that belong to other people, like friends and distant family. I'm a cat person, you see, but where I live currently has a no-pets rule.

My friend, Annie, asked me to house sit when she went on her holiday. Some months back, she'd acquired two new rescue dogs. Not at the same time. She'd gotten one to replace the dog that died of old age. Then, after a few weeks, the rescue center had begged her to take on another one. Lovely little animals these two were, she'd assured me. I was very happy to oblige, as it meant I'd get to enjoy Annie's beautiful garden.

Now, I had already met the pooches when I'd popped around to get keys and instructions. They were two dogs of indeterminate breed, each about one year old. Rascal, the little black one, had strong signs of the Scottish terrier about him. The other dog, Luna, had some Dachshund features and a glossy, tawny coat. Rascal had a perpetual look of curiosity and was as scruffy as Luna was smooth.

It was July, and that meant I was on a break from my academic job. The following weekend, I packed my bags cheerfully and drove off to Annie's house in the heart of Harfield Village.

"You need to be extra gentle with Rascal," she explained when I arrived. "He's been completely traumatized in his past life."

"By what?"

"I'm his fourth rescue mother," she admitted. "No one else could cope with him, so he's been moved around to several homes, the poor little thing." She gave him a cuddle, and he yapped happily. "Some people have no idea how to treat their animals."

"So, what does he do?"

"Well, he chews everything," Annie said.

I'd already noticed a few mauled dog toys scattered here and there.

"He's settled down quite a bit now. You just have to give him lots and lots of love and not leave him for very long."

Oh dear. This wasn't sounding too good.

"Really, I want you to enjoy your stay."

"What do I have to worry about, then?"

"Just don't leave shoes or nice clothes or books anywhere. Especially shoes!" She reiterated the instructions for meals, routines, and plant waterings. Then, we got to sleeping arrangements. "Sometimes Luna sleeps with me on the bed," she admitted.

"That won't suit me," I said. "I have allergies."

"They're very well-behaved," she insisted. "If they jump onto the bed, just push them off."

"They?"

"Well, not always both of them." Annie stared at me desperately. "Just shove them off."

Famous last words.

Well, my friends, I waved Annie off on her travels before settling in to read my book and chill. The dogs appeared content. They lay about in the garden while I read on the verandah. Then, I went into the kitchen to prepare their food and mine. After eating their supper with what I thought was unseemly haste, they looked at me hopefully as I proceeded to eat mine. They plonked themselves at my feet while I tried to watch television and stared at me through each and every excruciating morsel.

"I'm sorry, guys, but you've had yours."

More woeful stares. More heightened panting from Rascal.

"Curry is not good for you," I told them. "In fact, it can be very bad. Now, please, leave me in peace to enjoy my food." Feeling as guilty as a despot for not sharing, I struggled and choked my way through the meal while trying to figure out how to best get the dogs to be somewhere else at mealtime. I came up with nothing, so I braced myself for five days of feeling like the world's worst person whenever I ate anything. But then I hatched a plan: Titbits. Titbits would definitely mitigate the meal debacle.

On the first night, the dogs got into their beds obediently. I read for an hour and turned off the light. *This is going well*, I thought. *All very civilized.* I then fell into a deep sleep and had a horrible dream of being smothered.

I woke with a start. I was on my back, and I couldn't move. When I fully came to, I discovered I was being crushed by the two dogs lying on either side of me, dead to the world. I battled to loosen the duvet, but Rascal and Luna didn't budge. I felt trapped. I needed to get out of bed and drink some water. I tried to shift them gently, but this proved more of an effort than I was up to in my half-drowsy state. It felt mean to wake them up and shove them off the bed, so I wiggled and wriggled until I'd maneuvered myself to the middle of the mattress and could climb out over Luna.

Feeling quite grumpy, I made my way to the kitchen for a glass of water, only to turn around and see Rascal looking up at me eagerly, his tail thumping on the tiles with excitement.

"It's water, Rascal. Not food."

He looked at the coat stand where the leads hung and then back at me hopefully.

"No. It's the middle of the night. No walkies."

Well, I thought, *at least I won't have to negotiate the same terrain climbing back into bed as I did climbing out of it.* Rascal bounded joyfully ahead of me, waited for me to get in, and then jumped up to snuggle. Three sudden and enormous sneezes came upon me. He watched me closely with his big, watery eyes, without a modicum of guilt. I groaned, wondering how I was going to get through the night.

I must have fallen asleep at some point, because the next thing I knew, I was awakened by tongues licking my face. Two dogs were eager for me to get up and feed them immediately, if not sooner.

"This was meant to be my holiday of lie-ins and late mornings," I informed them in a stern voice. Then, sighing, I got up to feed the pooches and make some tea. I thought I might creep back to bed and drink it peacefully. It was Sunday, after all.

But they were both back on the bed before me. I stared at them for a moment. They stared right back at me. Accusingly. I settled myself reluctantly in the bedroom chair to drink my tea. I was going to have to have a serious talk with Annie about boundaries.

The smell of toast had the pair rushing to the kitchen half an hour later. By this point, I was in my tracksuit and ready to take them on their morning walk. It went well, all things considered.

What I haven't yet mentioned is that I was in a new relationship with this cute guy, Geoff, who taught music at the college where I worked. We'd been on a few dates that had gone well, so Geoff was coming to pick me up for a movie date. He arrived at six o'clock, and I buzzed him in.

"Did you find the place okay?" I asked, pecking him on the cheek.

"Yes, but parking's impossible here."

"Tell me about it."

Rascal was yapping loudly, and Luna was standing in front of Geoff, panting.

"Let me introduce you," I said. "This is Rascal and Luna."

He stopped to pet them both, and they seemed delighted to have someone new to sniff.

However, they weren't quite as delighted to see us both leave. Not at all.

"I won't be long," I told them. "Don't worry. Back soon."

"Not too soon, I hope," said Geoff, taking my hand and giving it a squeeze.

And we were off. I heard some barking as we drove past the house and hoped it would stop. They had water, food, toys, access to the back garden, and a bone each, per Annie's instructions.

We sat in the movie house with our popcorn and cokes, watching this story about Maggie Smith, who lives in a van and is sort of homeless, but the kind neighbor allows her to put her van in his driveway. It was lovely.

After the movie, we went to grab a burger before heading back to Annie's.

The house was eerily quiet as we approached. The dogs didn't bark as I turned the key, and I wondered why. I hoped nothing was amiss. Quite the contrary; they were standing there at the door like exasperated parents waiting to scold us for breaking curfew.

"Hello, my darlings." I bent down to give pets, realizing that I'd actually missed them. Luna seemed to have taken quite a liking to Geoff, but Rascal made his allegiance to me very apparent. Both seemed to forgive us quickly for abandoning them, but when I turned on the light in the lounge, I nearly had a heart attack. The place was a disaster. Every cushion had been savaged, and the entire carpet was covered with stuffing.

"What have you done?" I cried, my voice rising in alarm. I started trying, vaguely, to push some of the stuffing into the cushions and picked up what remained of one of my (previously) very expensive shoes.

Rascal, at least, had the grace to look ashamed. I hunted everywhere for the other shoe with no luck. Instead, gloopy tennis balls and half-gnawed, stinky dog bones lay everywhere. This room was not at all how I'd left it. Geoff watched me mutter and cuss to myself as I searched helplessly for my missing shoe. He was chuckling.

"You think this is funny?"

"Well, yes," he said, clearly enjoying himself. "It is."

"What am I going to tell Annie?"

"I don't think she'll be too surprised." Sensing my distress, he cleared his throat and allowed his smile to fade. "Where's that kettle? Let me put it on for us."

I directed Geoff to the kitchen where he had no trouble finding the kettle. I heard him bustling around, whistling quietly with Luna glued to his heels, as I gathered the worst of the chaotic stuffing into black plastic bags I'd found in the kitchen.

Rascal was uncharacteristically still. One of his ears was raised, and the other was at half-mast as he looked up at me with the saddest face I'd ever seen.

"Okay," I relented. "I'm going to stop being cross with you." I bent down to stroke him, and his tail started wagging. "This is my bad. I stayed out too long. I understand that you need to chew things when you feel anxious. We can fix this." It was while I was looking for a sewing kit that I noticed a folded note addressed to me:

Dear Di, if you are reading this, then Rascal has obviously attacked the cushions. Don't fret. The covers are recyclable. Anything precious is never left out. Love, Annie x.

A flood of relief washed over me as Geoff walked in with our coffee and placed the tray on the table.

"I found these shortcake cookies. Do you think your friend will mind?"

I smiled at him. "She'd better not. I'll deduct the cost from my shoe bill."

We sat down next to each other on the couch, and I grabbed a couple of nearby throws to roll into makeshift cushions. Geoff put his arm around me as we made ourselves comfortable.

I hardly noticed that the biscuits were disappearing very rapidly. I was feeding one to Rascal for each one of mine. Geoff was doing the same with Luna. At some point, two furry heads were resting on our respective legs until, finally, both dogs were fast asleep.

Neither one of us dared disturb them.

Diana Ashman is a semi-retired teacher who is passionate about her students. She has been writing since her school days and has had stories, articles, reviews, and poetry published in local magazines such as Darling, Femina, You, Drum, Tomorrow, *and* Writers and Readers Magazine. *Currently busy with two novels, she lives in Cape Town, South Africa.*

Brock

BY HIDAYAT ADAMS

BROCK WAS A BOSTON terrier, but he was no terror.

Sure, he was an ankle-biter with a weird bark—one that sounded like the hoarse screeching of a dying crow—but in reality, he preferred to avoid conflict whenever possible.

On the morning the little terrier met Dale, Brock was excited to go for his usual Friday afternoon walk through a place called the Green Belt. It was a lush stretch of nature trails through a sanctuary, and it was popular among dog walkers. Brock loved exploring there, especially since his owner, Justin, usually let him off leash once they were on the trail.

"Ready for your walk today, Brockie?" Justin asked as he opened the car door. Brock's favorite place was the passenger seat, right next to his tall, dark, and (in Brock's opinion) very handsome Master.

In reply, Brock wagged the tiny, stiff stump that passed for a tail. He gave Justin one of his doofus grins and settled comfortably on the seat.

"Listen. You'd better behave today, okay? One of my work colleagues is coming along with us, and he's a bit afraid of dogs." Justin was convinced the terrier understood every word he said. (Of course, he was right. It was humans who usually failed to comprehend dog language.)

Brock tilted his head. Somebody was joining them on their walk? The mildest tinge of annoyance smothered in a large dollop of envy crept along his spine. These Friday walks belonged solely to him and Justin. Who in the heigh-ho was this clown intent on invading their quality time? He shifted around in his seat as anxiety started to get a grip on his mood.

A few minutes later, Justin pulled up in front of Dale's house. When Dale approached the passenger door of the car, he found a tiny but feisty Brock giving him the double, protuberant evil eye.

"Gimme a sec, Dale," Justin said as he picked up the terrier, airlifted him to the back seat, and wiped off the front passenger seat with a cloth. "Brock's thrilled about the walk, but he's mad about being relocated."

Still standing outside, Dale peeked through the back window. Brock did not look at all like a thrilled terrier. In fact, he looked like a terrifying terrier ready to clamp his tiny teeth on Dale's face. "Err, you sure it's okay for me to get in?"

"Yeah, yeah," Justin assured him. "Brock won't do anything. He'll sulk, but he won't bother you."

That's what you think, Brock grumbled to himself.

"Okay, if you say so," Dale replied, still hesitant as he finally got into the car.

Brock kept his distance from the interloper. He tried climbing into the front seat a few times, but Justin scolded him and pushed him back.

"I feel really bad about taking his seat," Dale said after Brock's third attempt.

"Forget about it, man! He's just looking for attention. He's still technically a puppy, you know? Once we get to the walking trail where he can chase squirrels, he'll be fine."

Squirrels? Did you say squirrels? Brock's ears perked up as high as they could go (which wasn't very high, considering how small they were).

"Doesn't he bark?" Dale asked, looking back at Brock who was pacing back and forth now, clearly excited.

"Not really," Justin said. "Brock only growls when a large dog approaches him. I think it's because he feels intimidated, so he becomes aggressive to compensate for his lack of stature."

"Doesn't that mean the bigger dog will attack him?"

Justin laughed. "Nah. They usually look at Brock as if he's an amusing piece of fluff."

Hey! You should be defending me, traitor! Brock thought with indignation. *Just wait 'til we get home. I'll show you a piece of fluff.* With a soft *whuff* and plaintiff whine, Brock settled on the side behind the driver's seat. He enjoyed the smell of cigarette smoke that enveloped Justin like a second, invisible skin. To Brock, it was as natural as Justin's primary scent.

Once they arrived at the Green Belt, Justin opened the back door and clipped the leash onto Brock's collar.

Dale stared in amazement at the area through which they were about to stroll. "This is incredible! I can't believe I've lived here all my life and never knew about this beautiful place."

Lofty trees soared haphazardly all along a wide trail that meandered through a verdant mini forest. Tall reeds and grasses sprouted along the banks of a stream burbling merrily alongside the trail. Toward the center of the stream was a large pool with a wooden bridge across it. Some dogs romped gleefully in the water, their owners keeping a watchful eye on them from the bank. Brock tugged at his leash to be set free.

"Not yet, Brockie," Justin admonished. "Let's get a bit further in, then I'll unleash you."

Yeah, you'd better, or I'll pull your arm out of its socket.

Right then, three stocky, brown Scottish terriers approached. The smallest one sniffed Brock eagerly. *Nice bouquet,* he noted. *You had turkey kibbles this morning?*

Good morning ta ya, laddie, Brock greeted in his best brogue. Yes, indeed. *They were a bit dry, but I still enjoyed them.*

You're lucky, the Scottie replied as Brock butt-sniffed him. *We were fed blutwurst and sauerkraut. I hate that dish, but my missus thinks we live for blood sausages and fermented cabbage. Anyway, smell you later on our way back.*

"They were friendly," Dale remarked as the Scotties moved on.

Justin nodded. "Most of the dogs here are like that. It's why you'll find nearly all of them off their leashes."

"Seeing all these dogs in one place still unnerves me, Dale said, keeping close to Justin. "You know I'm not a fan."

Brock glanced back at the two of them and seethed. *You'd better keep your distance, Buster, or I'll have to take matters into my own paws and jaws.* A moment later, though, he sprinted off to investigate some enticing scents along the edges of the tree stands.

"Don't worry, Dale. They won't bother you."

As they reached the crest of the hill, Dale paused to gaze at the idyllic surroundings. On their left was a deep cleft in which some bamboo trees were growing, standing high and slender among a variety of other trees. Straddling the rift, like a natural bridge, lay an old, toppled oak. A flash of brown fur told Dale that a squirrel was cavorting among the branches, and he pointed it out to Justin.

Brock had been sniffing around some low-growing shrubs on the other side of the trail, but at the sound of the word 'squirrel,' he rushed over.

Where's that dang bushy-tailed rodent? he whined frantically. *Lemme at him!*

Justin grabbed hold of Brock's collar and pulled him away from the tree. "No, boy! Brock, get back!"

"Here, maybe he'll go for this," Dale suggested, picking up a stick from the ground. "Brock, fetch!" he shouted, throwing it as far as he could.

The terrier sprinted after the stick, but once he got to it, he merely sniffed at it and proceeded further up the path. *What?* he thought, trotting away from the humans. *You think I'm some stupid mutt who'll play this fetch game all day long? Puh-lease.*

"Sorry," Justin remarked, shrugging his shoulders at an amused Dale. "I should've told you: Brock doesn't fetch."

"You have one strange dog."

"Tell me about it."

Once they reached the end of the trail, they turned back. When they were about halfway to the car, Brock's attention was snagged by a beautiful, yellow Labrador retriever approaching them. Throughout the walk, he'd greeted other dogs, but he'd soon leave them to go exploring. With the Labrador, it was as if Brock was meeting a much-loved buddy.

"Ah, this is Brock's favorite pal," Justin said, smiling at the Lab's owner, a gray-haired lady in her sixties. "You know, I've been coming here with Brock for more than a month now, but I've never bothered to find out your dog's name," he told her.

Brock didn't need to ask her name. *Goldie!* he shouted, whuffing and snorting in delight.

While the humans made their acquaintances, the two dogs chatted it up as if they hadn't seen each other in years. The conversation was interspersed with licks, jumps, nips, and much flapping of ears.

The smells in this place are just the best, Brock enthused. *I nearly caught a squirrelly squirrel today!*

A squirrel? Where? Where? asked a thrilled Goldie, her tongue lolling.

Too soon, the humans decided to move on. Brock and Goldie touched noses one last time before going their separate ways.

Once they reached the car, Dale opened the front passenger door and stood back so Brock could jump inside. "I'll ride in the back," he said.

Stunned, Brock jumped up into his favorite spot.

"You don't have to do that," Justin insisted.

He was right. Brock stood at the edge of the front seat and leaned forward to give Dale's hand a swift lick before jumping into the back. *You're not too bad,* he thought. *I'll give you my favorite spot any time you want to come along for a walk.*

"Does that mean he likes me?" Dale asked, wide-eyed.

Justin grinned. "Yeah. I'd say he likes you."

You're welcome, Brock thought sleepily, curling up in a comfortable spot on the back seat as Justin started the car. The last thing he murmured before drifting off was *Let's go home, Dad. I'm hungry.*

Hidayat Adams has been an English teacher for more than 25 years. He hails from Cape Town, South Africa and is the self-published author of four short story anthologies and one fantasy novel. A self-described "indoor plant," he is currently writing a paranormal thriller.

SPECULATIVE
FICTION

Leader of the Pack

BY MICHAEL A. CLARK

"ARE YOU CHALLENGING ME, Staub?" Her tail rose.

"Maris, this doesn't concern—"

"It concerns The Pack. That's my business."

Her eyes were cold, January gray, far from the warmth of our last mating. She took a deliberate step toward me.

"Are. You. Challenging. Me?"

"I..."

"You're not answering my question."

"Maris, pulling your weight—"

"Is my job. As Leader of The Pack, I'll pull all the weight I want." Granite eyes, so arousing in heat, so chilling in power. "Now. If discipline needs dispensed, I will be the one doing the dispensing."

I'm her favorite mate. The soft nuzzling before we join, the gentle nips, the throaty growls. The wonderous conceiving of pups who will carry us through the old years.

I love her. Willful, inflexible Maris. A bitch of a leader. And a damn good one.

"Maris! Staub!" Stennett burst over a fallen pine log with puppling energy and skidded to a halt, kicking up some melting snow. "There's a bull moose two clicks over the left hill with a broken leg!" he panted. "Well, it looks broken...He's limping!"

Maris raised her nose north and squinted.

"More like two and a half clicks. But a moose there is."

"Well?"

She looked at me. "Looks like you're saved by the Hunt...again."

"Again?" I smiled. "I'll take Chambliss, Perry, and Nettles to the left."

"Good. Gamble, Spikes, and Hendrick with me," she said.

"Right."

"Then let's do it. We could stand to eat. And Staub, there's another scent in the air. Be careful."

We touched our noses and split off to lead our teams.

"Stennett, you're with me," I said. "Nice job picking up that moose spoor."

Stennett fell in line. "Thanks, boss."

Nettles gave him a stern look. "Just because you saw a moose dragging his foot doesn't mean he's hurt. Did he see you?"

Maris often let Nettles play drill sergeant with the young ones. But I was leading this hunt.

"Let him talk," I said.

We crossed a small brook edged in ice, with clear, cold water burbling over smooth stones. A hawk called through pine boughs hung low, just free of their winter frosting.

"Well...It's missing an antler. In a kinda marshy patch of ground, like where the beaver dam flooded that stand of aspen." Stennett walked with his head low, nose to the ground, unsure of himself.

"Which antler—left or right?"

"Nettles…" I said. There was a hint of prey in the breeze, along with the thousand other smells we could all ignore until they mattered. "Okay, Stennett. It was alone, right?"

"Yeah. Only other things around were a couple of voles and a porcupine. I think."

Bull moose missing an antler, maybe hurt…maybe not. Moose are as fast as we are on dry land, better in swamps. It'd be easier if it did have a broken leg, but taking down any moose is tough.

Maris's team was already circling toward the target. "Pick it up!" she called through the vast forest.

I led us through a small grove of willow astride a granite outcrop. Skunk cabbages were already bursting out of the new spring soil, and the first deerfly of the year buzzed past my head. I hate those damn things.

My nose was filling with moose scent, and the rest were picking him up, too.

"Staub. We've got company." Perry stopped and thrust his muzzle due west. He had the best nose in the pack and had saved our asses more than once.

"Bear?" I asked, fearing the answer.

"Yep."

"How big, and how far?"

"Big enough, and not too far. Less than a click or so west of the moose's spoor." Perry sniffed again. "Better tell Maris the bear will get to it before we do."

"Great." I howled through the forest.

"I know," came her reply. "Hurry your pups up, old man."

"Will do." I turned to my squad. "You heard the woman. Kick it up and be loaded for bear."

"Maybe we could swing left and get him between us and Maris," said Chambliss. He was average in a fight but had a knack for strategy.

"And if that bear gets to the moose first?" Nettles asked.

"Maybe we let him finish it off, and tire him out?"

"Good thinking, Chambliss," I said.

A badger hissed as we passed, black nose defiant from beneath a frost-draped log. We rarely trifled with them. Too many teeth and too little meat, with an attitude to match.

"Yeah, yeah, tough guy," Nettles said. "Go have a nice cold worm on me."

The badger hissed back into his burrow.

Closer now, the bear and moose spoor mingling in our noses along with the too-distant scent of our sisters, working their way around our target. We padded swiftly through the fading snow, over lichens already fresh and green.

"He's smelled us," Perry said.

"Damn. How close is he to the moose?"

"Too close. The moose has picked him up, too." Perry sniffed again. "It's not making tracks. The kid's right about it being wounded."

Stennett picked his head up. A little positive reinforcement never hurt anybody.

"Fan out," I ordered, and we deployed like we've done so many times before. Flowing smoothly through the trees and brush, silent and purposeful.

"Over that outcrop and past the stand of willows. He's...staying off the moose." Perry squinted.

"He knows we're coming and wants us to take it down so he can pick up the leavings," said Chambliss.

"Then he's a pretty smart bear."

"If he knows we smell him, and we go for the moose...?" Stennett asked.

Chambliss considered this. "We want him to do our work for us, right?"

"But if we draw him away so Maris can move in..." Nettles offered.

"That's how we'll play it," I said. "Nettles, Chambliss. Swing around that grove of pine on the left. Perry and Stennett, on my right."

I hoped the ground ahead would be flatter. Bears climb better than we do.

A couple minutes of fast loping, birdsong in the air. Small prey rustling in the cold, dry underbrush, thankful we were passing them by.

"He's swung back toward it," Perry said.

"Okay." I called softly to Nettles's team. "Get behind him and wait for my signal." Then, I yipped to Maris.

"Good tracking, old man. We're closing in. Be careful."

"Sound advice," I replied. A mole ducked into a hole a few feet away from me.

"Staub!" Chambliss shouted. "He's right in front of us!"

"What the hell—"

A booming roar tore through the woods.

"Here he comes!" Nettles barked.

"Let's go!" I commanded my team, and we flew over the small ridge that ran down from those pines our brothers had just crossed.

The bear was young and lean, cinnamon-brown with matted fur. His stomach lay in slack folds. He probably hadn't eaten for days.

We could take him. If Maris's troop brought down the moose, it would be worth it. Right?

"Staub, we're still a few minutes away. Don't engage that bear until I—"

"Just go for the moose!"

"Don't tell me what to do!"

"A little help here!" Chambliss shouted as the bear charged him. Amazing how fast something that big could move. Chambliss dodged the bear's jaws as Nettles growled behind him, waiting for an opening.

"Roll away!" I shouted as the bear swiped at Chambliss.

"Shit!" Chambliss caught most of the bear's massive left paw and went down.

Nettles lunged at the bear's flank, but the monster snapped back too quickly, and Nettles barely kept his nose on his face.

There were five of us and one of him, but he wasn't leaving us time to work our game plan.

In a flash, the bear spun toward me and charged.

As the alpha male and prime mate, I had a reputation to uphold. Unfortunately.

Sometimes, the best defense is a good offense. Questioning my sanity, I hurled toward the bear just as a thin, gray-and-white blur dove for its left hind leg.

Stennett got his young jaws around the monster's calf, and the bear bellowed in rage. It kicked, and Stennett's whole body snapped out like a pine bough in a thunderstorm. The brave kid held on for a split second more, then was flung aside, hard. But now I was on the bear's shoulder, and Perry and Nettles were hitting his left flank.

Bite deep, and yank left, then right. Rational thinking went by, as life and death were beyond words now. I got a mouthful of bear fur as he loomed like a living mountain. There was roaring in my ears and red behind my eyes.

What were Maris and I arguing about so long ago?

The bear shook like a stand of pines in a winter gale, and I went flying, hitting a fallen log hard. Thank God it was rotted, cushioning my fall.

The bear turned on Perry and Nettles. The latter went down with a swipe of a massive paw. Perry went for its throat; the sounds they made were blunt and terrible. I pulled myself to my feet and drove forward again.

This wasn't going well at all.

I hit the mammoth beast near its ass, hard enough to make its hindquarters slip and my vision blur. Out of the corner of my eye, I saw Stennett limp back toward the action. Good kid, full of guts. He'd get first of the choicest moose haunch tonight, if we all survived.

The pack lay about like beached whales in the fading light, gorged on moose. Tails twitching, noses buried in paws, sloth incarnate. I sluggishly rose to my feet and dragged myself to where Maris was starting to sleep off the feast.

"Good work," she said through slitted eyes, stretching out a paw.

"Yeah, but it hurt. Chambliss'll heal, but he won't hunt for a good week. Nettles is sore but okay. The kid's bouncing back like a champ."

"I like the way you're mentoring Stennett. Keep it up, and he'll be an alpha male someday."

"I'm not 'mentoring' anyone. Just trying to keep us all alive."

"Whatever you say." She rested her head on a moss-covered log. "We were arguing over something a while ago?"

"I can't remember what."

"Good answer." Maris yawned. "I'll be in heat soon. Think you'll be up to it again, old man?"

"I'll give it a shot."

"Love you," she murmured before dozing off.

"Love you, too," I said and settled down to the warming ground, happy for the chance to sleep with a full stomach and awaken with the coming spring light.

Michael A. Clark's work has been published in Galaxy's Edge, Mystery Weekly Magazine, Cosmic Horror Magazine, *and* Dark Matter Magazine, *Issue 016, among many other publications. His novella* Are One *has recently been published by Water Dragon Publishing.* "Whom the Gods Annoy" *has been published in Anotherealm, and his short story,*

"The Final Shot," appears at whitecatpublic ations.com/2024/04/09/the-final-shot/. Clark lives in Charlotte, North Carolina and currently works in industrial automation while spending as much time as he can outdoors. He likes baseball and writes short stories and music because that's what he does. He is feeling somewhat more confident about the future these days.

Brook and George

BY MARIAH SOUTHWORTH

I AM MY LADY'S protector.

When she loads the truck with her tables and boxes, I am there, guarding her back. I sit in the passenger seat as she drives, watching the other cars and sniffing the air. I sit by her side as she sets up her booth in the city, and I lay at her feet as she sells her pictures and sparklies to the people walking by.

I know I am big; people tell me so. My lady assures them that I am friendly, and I get lots of head pats and neck scratches. I don't need to bark and scare people, because I know I can protect my lady. I do not need to prove it.

There are lots of people at the market where she sells the things she makes. I watch them pass by with my curly head on my shaggy paws. I know all the smells of the market and the city: sweat, exhaust, food, asphalt, a rare whiff of raccoon, the dusty smell of pigeon.

When a stranger comes up with a basket of new smells, I pick my head up, ears cocked. The stranger and my lady talk, and my lady takes something white from the basket. I sit up. My lady kneels in front of me, her hands cupped around a ball of white fluff. Her face is full of joy and wonder. Realizing how important this is to her, I give the fluff a thorough sniff.

Two bright eyes look up at me, and a small, wet mouth opens. "Mrrow!"

I understand. This is my lady's baby, and I will protect him the same way I protect her. I start by washing his head.

My name is Brook. I know because my lady calls me that. Sometimes, she is hard to understand, but I can usually parse out what her noises mean when I pay attention, especially when her feelings are strong enough to smell.

The little ball of fluff is George. He is a cat, and we are a good girl and a good boy. It doesn't take George long to grow from a small ball of fluff to a large ball of fluff. George likes to sit on the bed and bat at me as I walk by. Then, I lick his fur, and he stares at me with shocked indignity.

The three of us live in a small house in the woods. When it's hot, my lady leaves the door open, and George and I come and go as we please. Sometimes George brings in dead birds, and sometimes he gets so full of burs that my lady spends hours picking him clean. I never cause such problems. In fact, I often improve the house by bringing in the interesting and wonderful perfume of the things I find to roll in.

George left early this morning. He hasn't come back yet, and his breakfast is still sitting in his bowl. It's lunch now, and my lady is so worried that she reeks of fear. This has never happened before. We walk all around our territory, calling for George. We even go down the hill and knock on the door of the Man-Who-Lives-At-The-Bottom-Of-The-Hill. George doesn't like him, and I'm not surprised when we don't find him there.

The day wears on, and still no George. It's summer, so the light lasts a long time. My lady spends all afternoon staring out the window. Finally, she looks at me. I can smell how worried she is, and I put a comforting paw on her knee.

"Brook," she says, her voice slow and serious. "Find George."

We stare at one another for a long moment. I stand. Yes, as the household protector, it is time for me to find our lost cat. Without wasting another moment, I trot out the door and begin sniffing for him. His scent is all around the house, but it is all old smells. Eventually, I fan out and find a recent trail heading into the woods.

I follow his path from that morning. He had stopped to sharpen his claws on an old stump. Farther along, he had relieved himself in a pile of dead leaves. He'd sprayed on a fallen fence post, and I very excitedly follow his scent parallel with the fence.

I smell blood in the air, metallic and strong. I freeze, my excitement turning into fear. I break into a run, following the fence line and the smell.

There's George, clinging to a tree trunk with his front claws, his white fur clotted with blood. He sees me and calls out with the smallest, weakest little meow I've ever heard. He doesn't move as I walk closer. I sniff him from head to toe, and I wince. The barbed wire from the broken fence has wrapped around his middle. The cruel barbs dig into his back and stomach.

Sitting, I whine deep in my throat. What do I do? I can't take him back with me. He's stuck. I can't go get my lady. Darkness has fallen, and already I can hear the rustle of the night prowlers. They smell his blood. George will not survive if I leave him.

My resolve hardens. I am his protector. I will do what I must.

The smell is a problem. Carefully avoiding the barbs, I begin to lick him clean. I can feel him trembling as I work the blood out of his fur, but he's too exhausted to protest. Once the smell is gone, I sit beside him and wait.

The creatures of the woods come. First the rats, with their red eyes and twitching noses. I pounce at them, catching one in my jaws and breaking it. The others flee in terror, and I toss the broken body into the bushes. Later, one of the lanky, wild dogs comes. I lift my head and growl. We stare at each other for a long time, but I am bigger, and he leaves, taking the body of the dead rat with him. Something big comes during the darkest part of the night. It smells of death and musk. I growl, hackles raised. The monster hesitates, then slinks away.

I keep the prowlers at bay all throughout the long hours, and whenever I smell blood, I lick George clean again. Eventually, the smells of the night give over to the the dawn, and the sun comes back.

Wearily, I sniff George. He smells alive, but he is cold and still. Worried, I lick his head. He opens his bright eyes and meows softly, once.

"Brook!"

I jump, head cocked. I can hear the underbrush rustling from far away.

"Brook!" It is the Man-Who-Lives-At-The-Bottom-Of-The-Hill.

I haven't barked since I was a puppy, but now I raise my head and bay loudly, the sound somewhere between a bark and a howl.

The crashing in the bushes grows louder, and the man appears.

When he sees George, his eyes widen, and he smells like fear. I let him get closer and show him just how dire the situation is. He pats my head and takes off running. I am too tired to follow, but we do not have to wait long. The man returns with his metal pincers in hand.

My lady follows him with a towel. She drops to her knees and hugs me, her face buried in my shoulder. "Good girl, Brook," she says. I lick her ear. She smells scared.

Using his pincers, the man snips the barbed wire holding George to the fence. He leaves it wrapped around George's stomach—he is afraid of more blood, perhaps? My lady wraps George in the towel, and we all rush home. The smell of my lady's fear lends speed to my tired body.

My lady takes George into her truck, leaving me to guard the house. I watch them drive away from the porch. Only when they are out of hearing and smell do I lay my head in my paws and rest.

George is back. He is inside the house, lying in a patch of sun. It's blinding on his white coat, what is left of it. He is no longer a fluffball; they shaved his entire middle and wrapped him in bandages. He is wearing a white cone, and there are tubes sticking out of him. He doesn't seem to mind, though. The medicine my lady gives him means he doesn't mind anything at all. That is fine. He has deserved his rest. I will protect him while he heals.

He is a good boy, and I am a good girl.

Mariah Southworth is a writer of horror, fantasy, and science fiction from the northwestern United States. When not writing, she is an elementary assistant teacher and playground storyteller. She has a deep love of mythology and history, and she incorporates this into her writing. Her short stories have appeared in a wide range of anthologies, and her self-published children's books are available on Amazon. For more information, visit her website at MariahSouthworth.com.

Puggy-Pooh

BY FIONA M. JONES

PUGGY-POOH SNUFFLED, MOUTH OPEN and tongue hanging out. He didn't like people; he didn't like shrill voices. But breathing was hard work for one of his breed, and he could never quite get enough air into his lungs to clear his head. Feeling dazed or confused always puts you at a disadvantage, and the survival instincts left over from another age told him to ingratiate. He wagged his stumpy tail.

"Oh, what a little cutie!" people cried. "Such a sweet-natured doggy. And what a lovely costume! Where did you buy it?"

"Oh, that," said Kortni, looking modestly downward. "It's homemade. A design I came up with when I was thinking about nature and stuff."

"Wow, you are so talented! He looks just like a real butterfly!"

Puggy-Pooh tried not to growl at the jiggling of his harness whenever anyone handled the wire wing-frames. A harness signified work, he knew from centuries of sled-dog lineage. One must submit, as to the leader of one's pack, keeping only a sideways eye open for the weakening of whoever wielded the power of the moment. He arched his back and then sneezed.

"Bless you! He's a beautiful little Puggy-Pooh, Kortni. You must adore him."

"Oh, yes," said Kortni. She kissed Puggy-Pooh on the nose, and he sneezed again as her perfume hit his sinuses.

He dragged behind her on his lead as they moved on. Waddling more and more slowly, he tried to catch his breath. A bitch had left her scent-mark at the base of the nearby lamp-post, but Puggy-Pooh couldn't read it. His nose, flattened by generations of selective breeding, felt thick and unwieldy, his sense of smell muffled by the flaccid folding of his breathing tract. He hung his mouth open wider, displaying crooked, asymmetric teeth.

"He's smiling!" someone said. There were always so many people along this street. Most of them seemed to know Kortni, and they always stopped to talk. "Who's a happy little doggy then? Who's got big brown eyes then? Oh, I love pug-dogs. If you ever decide to breed him, do let me know, Kortni. I'll be first in line for a new puppy."

Kortni nodded and bent down to scoop Puggy-Pooh up into her arms. They always ended their walk this way: Puggy-Pooh slowing to the point where Kortni could get home sooner by carrying him.

He wiggled a little, trying to reposition himself so as to see past his butterfly wings and out of his dominant eye. His brain had already learned to ignore the poorer-quality input from his squinted right eye and to decode his surroundings solely by the left. It was more efficient than deciphering the double vision caused by two eyes pointing in different directions. It added to his charm, of course. People went into raptures over the quizzical tilt of his head if he tried to focus on a toy or a dog treat.

People went into raptures no matter what Puggy-Pooh did. Bred for maximal appeal to the human psyche, he ticked every box for sheer cuteness: his helplessness; his small, squat body; his round, flattened face and bulged-out eyes.

"You know, I think she's right. I just might decide to breed you," said Kortni as she took off his harness inside the house. "You're so gorgeous, so perfect. People would pay pretty well for puppies like you, my Puggy-Pooh. I wonder how we'd go about it. I suppose I'll just talk to someone at the doggy club. There's that woman, what's-her-name, with a lady pug, and she's done puppies before. She uses them to pay for all her overseas holidays..."

Puggy-Pooh sniffled and squinted at the Lady Pug. She didn't smell of health or fitness, but something reminded him of the springtimes of previous lives. There had been many lives, many springtimes, many females whose scents he had understood better than this one. Best of all had been a lean-muscled, thick-furred female from a thousand years ago: a raw, wild, wolfish scent—strong, fierce, and promising. There had been puppies, and they had survived the harshest winter under her provision, for she could hunt like a ghost and kill like a knife. Her blood, running in and out of two hundred different lives, still ran in his veins and gave him something like hope. He shuffled toward the Lady Pug and stood his ground as she turned and snarled her disapproval.

Yapping hoarsely, he tried to approach again, to tell her what he remembered, but the Lady Pug had been washed in floral shampoo—a smell that belonged to shrill-voiced humans, not to wolves. Also, she was unwell: there was something like the smell humans had when they said "diabetes." Puggy-Pooh struggled to breathe in more deeply, to untangle one scent from another, but he was already tired from the car journey across town to the Lady Pug's home.

"Um," said Kortni. "Are you sure she's actually in season? I mean—"

"Sorry," said Enia, the other owner. "We can try again tomorrow, if you like? I'll give her a little sedative; that's what I had to do last time. Honestly, I'd love her to have a litter from a pure-breed like Puggy-Pooh. They'll sell like hotcakes."

"If it doesn't work..."

"Look, if all else fails," said Enia, "there's always artificial insemination. You know, a lot of these pure-breeds have, er, trouble, physical fitness and all that. It doesn't cost that much, all things considered."

"Okay," said Kortni. "Yes, artificial actually sounds good to me. If it doesn't work, like, the natural way, of course."

"Sure. We'll get our puppies, one way or another. Don't you worry."

Cold air blew in through the open doorway that evening as Kortni carried out the usual black plastic bag: rubbish, food wrappings, and Puggy-Pooh's unwanted dinner. "I hope you're not ill, my dear," she fluted at him on her way past. "'Cos we're going to do it again tomorrow, aren't we, with that pretty little Lady Pug?"

Puggy-Pooh shivered. He had never liked the nighttime, the darkness, the cold wind without his frilled and padded coat. It was harsh, like the lives and deaths of half-forgotten generations before him. He stared, arose, and went to look. Beyond the acidic, electric beams of the streetlights was a round, white moon that he recognised like a long-lost friend.

He padded outside, hardly even wheezing now as the thin cold air dilated his airways and awakened his heart and lungs. He had never walked outside by himself before. He would follow the moon for a while, find out where it led him. He would search for new smells and sounds to see if he could make sense of them. He would return in the morning, perhaps. Kortni and her voice and her perfume would never notice he had been away.

The moon held steady in its position, trustworthy, like a tree or a gatepost. It had always been there; it always would be. It led Puggy-Pooh out of town and across the fields, up a hill, and across a road toward dark trees that seemed to reach and gesture in the way humans could never quite do correctly. Puggy-Pooh understood and obeyed, no longer feeling afraid. He walked slowly, smelling the altered chemistry of night, thinking of the strobing of nights and days upon the living world with its cycles of memories, of lives.

The glare of a speeding car took him almost by surprise: a momentary blinding, a deafening, a sense of shock. In an instant, the night opened wide. It was no longer empty like a dark room but full, like deep water. He was running now, faster and longer in stride than he'd ever run before, sliding through undergrowth and between trees like a shadow, the moon still blinking at him, showing him the way. The forest was full of shadows, and they were alive.

Something had fallen off him, he wasn't sure what. Something irrelevant, like a ruffled collar with an electronic tag. An illness, a slowness. A name, forgotten, as though it had only existed many years ago. He felt as light as air or moonshine. The running shadows threaded in and out of one another like the waters of a river—or the flow of lives and deaths. He was here and there, in one place and then in another, searching for the life he would remember best, and the companion whose memory had never quite deserted him.

He would find her, the one who could hunt like a ghost and kill like a knife, and before the morning came, she would remember him, too.

Fiona M. Jones writes short dark-themed fiction, nature-themed CNF and, sometimes, poetry. Links to her published work can be found on her website: FionaMJones.wordpress.com

Junie and the Crow

BY BOB SMITH

JUNIE AND THE CROW were at odds from the beginning.

Their feud started the day Junebug came home to the farm and instinctively headed toward the dumpster on the property to see if there were any treats to be had. How could she have known there was a crow in there who was already shopping? Though neither would admit it, they both nearly had a heart attack when Junie jumped in.

And so it went every day after that unfortunate meeting: a shrill *Ka-Caw, Ka-Caw* from high up on the wire, followed by an ear-splitting *Bork* from down below. The jabs and putdowns they'd trade after that were always the same:

"Hey, ground-dweller," the crow would taunt. "You're the funniest looking bird I've ever seen. Where are your wings?"

"Look who's talking," Junie would bark in retort. "If I had a nose like yours, I'd put my head in a hole."

In fact, the two looked very much alike in some ways, with the shiniest, blackest coats you've ever seen. Neither had ever asked what the other one was; both assumed the other was just a funny looking version of themselves.

At first, the other animals on the farm enjoyed the spectacle. They even goaded the two occasionally, like kids on the playground. But, like anything else, the feud eventually grew old until even the wild bunnies tired of it.

Still, whenever they crossed paths, the adversaries would pick up where they'd left off.

"You're a dirt bird," the crow would tease.

Pawing at the ground like a bull, Junie would reply, "Why don't you come down here and say that to my face?"

Inevitably, the crow would take things too far, hitting below the belt. "It's no wonder your mom pushed you out of the nest," he said one day in late summer.

This hurt Junie deeply, for she had been abandoned at a truck stop by her first family. And while her new family loved her and took good care of her, Junie never forgot the hard lessons of living on the streets and in the shelter...

One day, in her old life, Junie had found a storm drain behind the truck stop. She'd had to evict a skunk who was living there to get it (and she'd paid a hefty price for that encounter), but at least she'd had a den afterward.

It didn't take her long to learn the evening trash schedule. Hopping up into the dumpster, she'd carefully rip open the bags humans brought out from inside the truck stop. She'd usually look right past the French fries, which just made her thirsty, in search of her beloved cheesy paper. Occasionally, humans would see her and begin to approach, but the lingering skunk smell kept them at a distance.

At night, Junie would dream of a home of her own, with a warm, soft bed and belly rubs. There would be all the clean, fresh water she could drink and her own bowl full of kibble. Waking up to the sounds of trucks rumbling past, she'd make a halfhearted attempt to groom her once-beautiful coat, which was now matted and filthy.

Junie did pretty well (she was a survivor after all), but she was getting thin and weak. The desert sun made her thirsty like never before, and she grew desperate. It had been a few days since she'd last found something to drink when she came across a puddle. It looked like a melted slushy, glossy and shimmery. Junie had drunk slushies before; she'd learned to pay close attention to the little people walking behind the big people, because they dropped things all the time.

In a moment of despair, she tried a little of this new puddle. It tasted sweet. Driven by tormenting thirst, she threw caution to the wind and lapped the rest of it up, not knowing it was antifreeze which had spilled from a car. Almost instantly, she felt wobbly and dizzy, and then everything went black...

"You're a very lucky dog," said a voice as a hand reached through silver bars to scratch her behind the ears.

Coming back to consciousness, Junebug realized some fur was missing from her leg, and she was connected to a tube. Normally, she would panic and try to escape, but she was too weak to do either.

Opening the door of the holding pen and placing a collar around her neck, the man said, "We have to give you a name now, don't we? Well, looking at the calendar, and since the truck stop manager said you only came out at night, let's call you Junebug."

Junie instantly liked the sound of it. She also liked having a collar again and the scratches behind her ears; they reminded her of her first family.

Life in the shelter turned out to be such a mix of opposites that she wasn't sure if this was heaven or prison. After all, there were two meals a day, plenty of fresh water, and the people that came and went all looked at her with kindness and concern. On the other hand, there was no soft bed—she was in a kennel on cold concrete with just a blanket—and some of the dogs there never stopped barking and threatening her.

Eventually, Junie settled into the rhythm of shelter life, nonetheless. She even made some friends in the yard. She began to put on weight and had several baths, so her coat was starting to shine again. Being smart, she noticed when some of the other dogs—especially the puppies—would leave with people who came to walk the aisles and look into the kennels. Junie couldn't help but wonder if it would ever be *her* turn to leave the shelter.

Then, one day, everything changed. It started with a few things Junie had been through before. They'd bring her in from the yard, and the people would be nice to her, but then they'd leave with another dog. This time, Junie was going to play it differently: Instead of smiling and wagging her tail like she usually did when she was brought back inside from the yard, she collapsed on the floor with all four legs splayed out like overcooked linguini. With her nose on the linoleum, she stared at the human's feet and saw black boots. Curious, Junie began scanning upward. She saw black pants, a black jacket, and long, shiny black hair. She was astonished at how much this person looked exactly like her. *This must be my person,* Junie thought.

Indeed, it was. In what felt like a whirlwind of motion, she was in the back seat of a car heading to a new home.

As she explored the farm, Junie had no way of knowing that her new family kept her on the leash out of fear she might run off and get hit by a car before she could fully acclimate to her new home. The farm was huge and peaceful. There was even a dog door where she could come and go as she pleased, and there was a giant, warm bed and a food dish just for her. There were animals of every kind on the farm, including skunks, but Junie knew to stay away from them. Unlike at the shelter, all the animals got along the best they could, and everybody had their place, even the gophers. Junie settled in quickly.

Still, certain habits from those tough times in her past died hard. Whenever her water dish at the farm was filled, for example, Junie would try to drink all of it at once, because she never knew when she might happen upon fresh water again. And the first few times her new mom said it was time for din-din, Junie headed to the dumpster near the barn, because that's where her dinner used to come from at the truck stop. She'd especially treasured the dumpster delicacy known as cheesy paper—the outer wrapping used to hold what she'd heard the truckers call 'cheeseburgers.' To Junie, that paper was heaven on earth. Unfortunately, if mom ever caught her with it, there was no doubt in Junie's mind she'd take it away, just like she'd once taken away an elk bone Junie had found fair and square. There was no use in worrying about such a thing, though: Junie didn't live near a truck stop anymore, so it was unlikely she'd ever taste cheesy paper again.

Junie hadn't seen much of the crow since their last confrontation, but his words still stung when she thought about them, especially that last hurtful remark about Junie's mother pushing her out of the nest. Junie vowed to get even one day.

As it happened, that day was a grey, blustery afternoon in the fall. True to her routine, Junie went outside to have her post-breakfast zoomies. She had regained her full strength; she was fast, agile, and shiny once again. As she ran, something on the ground by the back fence caught her eye. It, too, was shiny and black.

Cautiously, Junie moved in to investigate. As she crept closer, she saw that it was the crow and that he was snagged in a piece of plastic packaging. Knowing this was her chance to get even, Junie pounced on her startled nemesis with all her might. Expecting to relish the moment, she was surprised to be struck with an instant feeling of pity when she saw terror in the crow's eyes. Seeing the crow trapped and afraid reminded her of life at the truck stop and the shelter.

The crow, for his part, appeared resigned to his fate and braced for the worst.

Junie, however, had experienced a sudden change of heart. "I should eat you," she said with a playful but still slightly sinister tone. "You know that, right?"

The crow, trying to breathe under the tightness of the plastic wrapped around his neck and wing, simply nodded.

"You don't know what it's like to be trapped, to be locked up, do you?" Junie asked him as she relaxed and began to peel the plastic away with her teeth.

To the crow, it felt like an eternity with Junie's hot breath and giant white canines so close to his throat. Finally free, he struggled to understand the monumental change that had just taken place, with Junie helping him instead of tormenting him. As the plastic blew away, the crow stood up and inspected himself for injuries.

Junie felt the need to defend her street credentials. "I know what it's like out there," she said. "I used to live out of a dumpster, after all."

The crow looked at her, incredulous. "What are you talking about? I love dumpster diving. Remember that first day we met, when you almost jumped in on top of me?"

Junie nodded once. "I do. So, just what in the world were you doing with all of that plastic, anyway?"

"I can't help it," he responded with a small shrug. "I can't resist shiny things." And then, just like that, the moment was over, and the crow flashed away in a cloud of dust.

After this remarkable event, there was no sign of the crow at the farm. The wild bunnies even asked, from a safe distance, if Junie had seen him. Junie began to long for their old banter, and she worried that the crow might have gotten trapped again. A part of her understood his absence: After all, if word ever got out among the crow's friends that a ground-dweller had saved his life, his reputation would be toast.

The days stretched into months, and life resumed its placid schedule at the farm. True to Junie's afternoon routine, the warm spring sun found her napping by the woodshed. Sensing someone watching her, Junie looked up and spotted the crow high in the sky. Sitting up, she watched as the crow descended in lazy circles, looking more like a vulture than her old nemesis. Happy and relieved to see him, Junie noticed something in his claws.

The crow never landed. Instead, he made a low pass over the horse pasture and released the item before flying away.

Riddled with curiosity, Junie ran to intercept it. As it floated down toward her, Junie realized what it was: It was cheesy paper—real, honest-to-goodness, fresh-from-the-dumpster cheesy paper. As it landed, she lay down in the dirt, framing her prize in between her front paws.

Junie was so transfixed by the unexpected presence of her favorite delicacy that she failed to notice the sound of a familiar pair of black boots approaching from behind. Before she realized what was happening, Mom's hand reached for the cheesy paper.

"Sweetheart," she said as she took it away. "You'll make yourself sick on this."

Noooooooooooo, Junie howled.

Bob Smith is an Arizona-born Norwegian who first worked as pastry chef at the Ritz Carlton in the 80s. He was on the forefront of the mountain bike revolution while he earned a BS in Public Relations at Northern Arizona University in the 90s. As a recently retired Sergeant Deputy Sheriff, he continues to cultivate a love for all things creative. Now, as an RV enthusiast, he can be found on YouTube as Yeti at Large.

Baby Steps

BY JAKE STEIN

BABY ISN'T ALLOWED TO go outside.

Every night, she paws the sliding glass door, craving the moon and stars, imagining how the cool wind would feel against her fur. The darkness beckons her; Baby wants to be free of this confined space where she has already investigated every shadowy corner, every dusty nether region under furniture, and has found—for ages now, it seems—nothing left to discover.

There is, however, a single exciting thing which occurs in this house: One of the humans, the one called David, will often pour milk and food into Baby's bowls.

At first, Baby laps thirstily...but the milk begins to taste sour from routine. She wishes more than anything that she could find somewhere fresh to explore—she suspects the world beyond these walls is huge, possibly endless. But the humans are ever-so-careful when they open the door, blocking any chance of escape with their massive legs. So, Baby is stuck here with the usual nooks and crannies and boring old milk.

David touches softly, and his noises are gentle, but the other human—her name is Yuna—never plays with Baby. Then again, she doesn't appear to play with David, either. Yuna mostly stays in the room at the end of the hall; sometimes, when David joins her, there's shouting and crying. Other times when they're both in there, it's perfectly silent, which is even worse.

Baby doesn't understand why the humans fight. They are free, after all, with the power to go outside at any time. What should David and Yuna have to complain about? Their arguments follow the same patterns: "One step at a time, honey," David will always say. "Just remember what the doc said. If this treatment doesn't work, we still have options."

Baby suspects that, somehow, she is causing the tension. Because the biggest shouting match so far was the very first one Baby witnessed, which occurred weeks ago when Baby was originally emptied from a pet-carrier onto the rug of this house. She recalls David telling Yuna, "Don't name her that. It's just cruel to yourself." Baby doesn't want to believe this was David and Yuna's first argument, but she will never know for sure.

And how can a name be cruel? Humans are so confusing, especially David.

Yuna, on the other hand, isn't complicated; Baby senses in this female a kindred feeling of being trapped and not understanding why. Baby almost even catches herself developing sympathy for Yuna...until the woman declares, amidst one of her customary eruptions, "Stop whining, Baby! No, you can't go outside! You're too small! Do you want to get eaten by a hawk?"

Baby doesn't know what a hawk is, but judging by Yuna's tone, the hawk isn't really the issue. Maybe Yuna keeps Baby inside for the same reason she locks herself in her room: She's just unhappy. Maybe, if Baby can cheer her up, Yuna will let her out.

Baby tries and tries, nudging and licking Yuna for a pet, a laugh, or at least a smile. But for all her efforts, Yuna evidently doesn't find her adorable. "I just wish you were enough," the crying woman tells Baby, though she may actually be telling herself, or even David.

One night not long after that, Baby is staring at her own reflection in the sliding glass door. It's the reflection of a small and pathetic thing. She feels crushed beneath Yuna's sadness—one emotion which puppies simply aren't equipped to tolerate. Baby wishes she was bigger, wishes she was...enough.

Well, sometimes, wishes come true.

It begins with a tingling in her nose. The sensation travels through her face and then into her neck. It ripples down her spine until every bone is burning, then freezing, then... bloating? Now her skin is stretching, her fur getting longer, her insides stirring. The transformation—her sudden growth spurt—doesn't hurt. But it does scare Baby. It scares her worse than thunder.

In her panic, she crashes through the door. An explosion of broken glass. Still, no pain.

She glances around at the shattered door, its pieces sparkling like starlight on the ground; she is shocked by her own strength. It registers with a heavy thud of her heart that she made it outside.

Screaming from another room. Hurrying footsteps. The humans. Baby has a choice: Run away or go back inside.

A cool gust of wind tickles her ears, and there's nothing left to consider.

Bounding away on powerful limbs, Baby hurtles through the night. She jumps a fence, then clears an entire tree in a single leap. When she lands, her mighty haunches shake the earth. She howls with delight—a wonderful, ear-ringing blast—and takes off in a random direction. She is so big that nothing can stop her. She breathes in freedom, and the open darkness—the gaping, infinite openness of the world—warms her eyes.

It isn't until she makes it to the woods that she realizes she's still growing.

Trees snap at her slightest touch. The moon and stars seem to be falling, getting closer. Baby has never experienced such pure capability. With every step, a thunderous quake and a rising cloud of dust. And then...

...a crunch, followed by more screaming from far below. Baby lifts a paw, sees a little house...which she just flattened. An ant-sized human is running away. For a second, the screaming man sounds like David.

Baby doesn't want to crush any Davids.

She lets the tiny man get away before continuing to roam, more carefully now. She discovers a wide river, which she is happy to drink from, but the water is icy and makes her shiver. She finds herself missing the taste of milk.

She realizes she'll never be able to go back to Yuna and David. She is simply too massive. At least she has plenty to explore, an entire world full of strange places, but Baby is surprised to miss the familiar comfort of a certain house she'll never fit into again.

She steps easily over the wide river and resumes wandering the unending gloom of the cold, empty world...no, not so empty. A distant noise, getting closer: a humming, a whirring. Baby notices an animal dipping out of the clouds. Or is it an animal? It looks unnatural, too shiny, with wings that don't flap. There's another noise, followed by flashes of light and a stinging pain, like an insect bite.

Panicked, Baby runs. She doesn't want to get stung again. But the flying thing chases her. This must be one of the "hawks" Yuna mentioned. Is this the sort of thing outside dogs have to deal with? Attacks from the sky? If only Baby had known it would be like this. In her haste, she stumbles over a small mountain and lands heavily in a valley. The so-called "hawk" doesn't give up; it stings her again by spitting at her.

Go away! Baby swats at the buzzing thing with her huge paw, but misses. Then she is back to running as fast as she can. Panting, hurting. Why did she ever want this? She wishes she'd never grown so big. *Can I be small again, please? As small as I once was?* She wishes, wishes hard...

And while it is rare, wishes do occasionally come true twice in a row.

Baby feels it first in her bones, a tightening. Suddenly, the trees appear to get taller. Yes, she is shrinking—she is shrinking! And the hawk...is becoming a giant.

But now, Baby can hide.

She squeezes inside the hollow of a tree, letting the cozy darkness hug her until, eventually, her huge winged enemy gives up its search and flies off. Baby stays in her hiding place for a while, filling herself with the solace of snug safety even after she's sure the hawk is gone for good. Why did she ever take enclosed spaces for granted? Why didn't she realize how wonderful it is to fit inside somewhere?

To be a part of something.

Her legs seem to know the way. It's a long, long journey, and Baby figures it's hopeless; they'll never take her back. But she has nowhere else to go.

Hopping the fence is harder when you're small, but Baby finally succeeds, landing in the yard with the broken door and the familiar house. Well, not so familiar from the outside.

For much of the night, Baby hides behind a tree and watches the house, the peaceful stillness, the quiet of this place, where the moon and stars are perfectly far away.

It's not completely quiet though.

Pricking her ears, Baby can faintly hear someone crying within the house. She recognizes Yuna's sobs, and she remembers that this place is not without its own pain.

David appears in the broken doorway. He looks around, and Baby wonders if he could possibly be looking for...her?

Yuna joins him. She holds something in her hands—a bowl.

"It's probably no use," David tells her. "She's got to be long gone by now."

But Yuna doesn't listen to him. She sets the bowl down outside, and Baby catches a whiff of milk. "I just wish..." Yuna says softly.

And, while it's very rare indeed, wishes do sometimes come true three times in a night.

Baby steps timidly out from behind the tree, her tail twitching.

Then, for a time, it's not quiet at all; the humans become very loud, but it's a nice loud. Yuna even picks her up. Yuna! Has Yuna ever played with Baby before? Well, she is playing with her now. Or, no, something better. Yuna is snuggling her. And smiling—smiling!

Deep inside Baby's small body, she feels a pang of victory. Somehow, it seems, she has made Yuna happy after all.

As it happens, Baby doesn't stay small forever. She becomes pleasantly plump, in fact. But she never gets nearly as big as she grew on that strange night when too many wishes came true. This suits her fine because Yuna doesn't cry anymore.

These days, the humans even play together sometimes. Baby would like to think she deserves some credit for that. But she also knows their joy springs from another wish that ended up coming true, in the form of a third human who joined the house—a smaller one, much slower and louder, who cries often and walks on four legs, like Baby.

And even though nobody stops Baby from going outside anymore, she sticks to the yard. Better to take the world one familiar place at a time, she figures, even if you don't get very far.

Jake Stein currently survives in Portland, Oregon, where he concocts strange tales on his laptop and spends too much time in Powell's Books. His work has appeared or is forthcoming in Lightspeed Magazine, Ellery Queen Mystery Magazine, *and* The No Sleep Podcast. *You can occasionally find him fumbling around Twitter/X: @jakewritesagain*

SCIENCE
FICTION

Alien's Best Friend

BY RICHARD LAU

THE BOY OF TEN squinted up at the transient man who loomed above him like a towering sundial casting an ominous shadow.

The man knew he struck an imposing figure, for he drew his likeness from the cigar store Indian statue outside of the laundromat: stern, sharp features, night-black hair, copper-toned skin, and even the fringed deerskin pants and vest (if anyone noticed the similarity between the wooden sculpture and the image his belt device projected, they didn't say anything). He and the dog were just two more oddities in a small town full of characters.

Nobody remembered, or cared about, when they had appeared.

Townsfolk referred to the pair as "Six Legs," for they seemed inseparable. They clearly shared a special bond, sometimes just staring at each other as if engaged in a silent conversation. Individually, they were called "Two Legs" and "Four Legs" (if the town's inhabitants ever saw the man's real form, they'd have to multiply his name by four).

"Can I throw the ball for your dog?" the boy asked.

"It's not a ball." Two Legs watched the boy's expectant expression change to one of disappointment, so he quickly added, "But you can throw it."

The boy's face lit up again, and the dog gave a happy bark, dancing in small leaps in a circle.

Two Legs handed over the orb. He watched the boy examine its glittering surface, a mosaic of metal and glass.

"It's like a disco ball!" the boy exclaimed, the reflections of light spotting his face like sunlight sparkling off a pond. He moved his arm up and down, amazed at the orb's seemingly fragile, feathery weight and contradictory sturdiness. Then he threw it.

As the spherical object flew through the air in a short, shallow arc, Two Legs remembered a day long ago.

He'd worked with a planetary exploration team, sending orb probes through small portals to other worlds. The orbs were supposed to take quick measurements and return. However, this one hadn't.

Still, the orb's readings made it back through the portal and into the attended monitoring devices. Two Legs, or Gabloq as he was known back then, could see that the external environment and atmosphere were tolerable to his kind. From the received images, the area seemed to be populated by giant plants resembling larger versions of Gabloq's people. However, these individuals of leaf and bark seemed largely stationary, lacking mobility with their lower legs rooted into the ground. They also did not seem particularly sentient. He would learn later that these plants were called 'trees.'

Being young and impetuous, he announced, "The probe's position is right outside the portal. I'll just hop over and pick it up." Before his seniors could stop him,

Gabloq grabbed a portable personal image projector, toppled through the opening, and...unintentionally initiated a first-contact situation.

On the other side, a creature awaited. It wore a dried-skin collar with a metal tag hanging from it. Gabloq knew minor species didn't typically adorn themselves with jewelry; the creature was obviously one of this planet's dominant, intelligent lifeforms.

And it carried the orb in its mouth.

Gabloq immediately activated the personal image projector in camouflage mode and faded from view, but the creature still seemed to detect him—perhaps not visually but by some other method. Wagging its tail, it pressed a wet nose to Gabloq's root tips, causing them to curl away like uncovered worms suddenly exposed to sunlight. Gabloq scuttled away from the portal, trying to hide behind a nearby lamppost.

The creature followed, but it was now distracted, sniffing the rusted metal base of the post. In an effort to communicate, the creature chose to produce a liquid chemical message that puddled around Gabloq's roots.

Feeling that his presence had been discovered—and trying to make the best of the situation—Gabloq tried to return the message, releasing his own liquid stream, concentrating on the words for 'peace,' 'mean no harm,' and 'friendship.'

The creature yelped and ran a few steps away (obviously, some improvements in communication were needed).

It was then that Gabloq realized the portal had closed behind him. It must have been a mechanical failure or interference between the two planets: His people would certainly not abandon him here!

How long ago was that? Two Legs wondered.

The boy was throwing the orb again. His arm seemed weak and uncoordinated. Two Legs had seen him with other boys his age, usually trailing behind them and often an observer, rather than a participant, in their games. There was such a thing as natural human talent, Two Legs knew, but how could one improve without practice?

So, when the boy offered the orb back to him, Two Legs said, "Are you sure you don't want to keep throwing? Four Legs is certainly enjoying it, and I can use the rest."

The boy grinned, and Two Legs retreated into the shade of a nearby redwood. The tree reminded him of an out-sized version of his mother, who he greatly missed. He respirated slowly to, once again, consider the past.

There was nothing Gabloq could do about the absent portal, but he could try to mitigate the exposure of his first contact. He switched his image projector to mirror an upright being standing by a distant fountain. Perhaps this new form would throw off the creature confronting him?

Unfortunately, the change in appearance only seemed to excite the creature further. It dropped the orb at his feet, an obvious peace offering, and emitted a sharp, hap-py-sounding bark.

Gabloq picked up the orb to examine it. It was covered in some slippery fluid from the creature's mouth—per-haps this was the reason the orb's self-propulsion sys-tem shorted out? In anger and frustration, he threw the now-useless device away, forgetting that he should prob-ably retain all technology foreign to this planet.

To Gabloq's embarrassment, the creature obviously knew the rules of first contact better than he, for it went and retrieved the orb once more.

"I don't want this piece of junk," he complained, hoping his tone would convey the meaning his words could not. "It's what brought me here, and it won't help me get home." He threw the orb again, harder this time. The contest turned into a battle of wills, but after the first few throws, Gabloq found himself relaxing and actually enjoying the activity.

The boy was throwing better, his natural ability seeping through like the sweat through his t-shirt. As the sun began to set, he glanced at his watch and grew sullen. "I gotta go home for dinner. Can we play fetch again tomorrow?"

Two Legs nodded. When they shook hands, Two Legs received a burst of mental imagery and information from the boy. Hope always came through most clearly.

As the boy was walking away, he turned and said, "My name is Kevin, by the way."

"Nice to meet you, Kevin. We're—"

"I know," said Kevin.

Later that evening, Six Legs enjoyed some charitable scraps from the kitchen of McMillan's Sports Bar. The owner was a friendly, talkative fellow, so Two Legs said, "Tell me about this game called baseball."

That night, in their secluded, sheltered spot in the park, Four Legs slept as Two Legs squeezed the baseball McMillan had given him. He thought about home plate and going home.

As summer progressed, the bond between Two Legs and Kevin grew to the point where Two Legs could easily pick up thoughts and images from the boy's mind. He was amazed at how much Kevin seemed to be a stranger in his own world. Granted, the boy didn't have Two Legs's training in adapting to foreign cultures, his technology, or his telepathic abilities to help with learning unspoken social customs and accepted behaviors.

Two Legs thought of his bond with Four Legs. Through that bond, he'd learned that Four Legs had previously been assigned the name of 'Rover' by a family of bipeds that had since moved away, abandoning the creature. It was hard to believe that these uprights were the dominant species with such callous behavior. Rover's breed was known as a 'German shepherd.' Perhaps most importantly, Two Legs learned that it was considered highly improper for uprights to leave liquid chemical messages in public.

He wished he could give Kevin some of these advantages, a gift of insight in understanding and being accepted by his peers. Two Legs now realized that Kevin had approached him out of sheer loneliness and desperation.

"Do you have any baseball equipment?" asked Two Legs one day, as if reading Kevin's mind.

Kevin shifted awkwardly. "A bat and a glove. But I haven't used them much."

"Bring them tomorrow."

What's this new thing we're doing? Rover's question appeared in the dog's eyes and in Gabloq's mind. *We don't play fetch as much as we used to. Not you and me. Not me and the boy.*

Gabloq admired that Rover's species seemed to only inquire about the really important things, such as food, shelter, and care. Concerned, he answered the dog's question with one of his own. *Are you upset?*

Rover shook his head. *My species doesn't get upset about things like that. I'm happy for your sense of accomplishment when the boy does well. I'm happy when he's happy with his own achievements. And I'm happy being here with the two of you. We dogs are very simple in our outlook.*

Gabloq tried his best to project what he felt was Kevin's need. *I'm teaching him to pitch. The boy needs to practice playing catch with others of his kind.*

Rover tilted his head to the side. *But you're not his kind.*

No, sadly I am not. But I'm the closest he has. Gabloq playfully scratched the dog behind the ears. *Unless you want to learn to throw?*

Rover's answer was simple: *I'm strictly chase and catch.*

Well, I will be teaching Kevin how to bat soon. If you're patient, you can chase the balls he hits.

Great!

By the end of summer, Kevin was, for once, looking forward to the start of school. Thanks to Six Legs, he had new skills to impress the kids during recess and P.E. He was confident that he would win some friends, but if he didn't, he no longer felt he needed to.

"They're going to start calling us Eight Legs and a Golden Arm!" Two Legs teased him.

The other kids in the park had noticed Kevin's throwing and hitting ability. Already, they wanted to play with him.

Two Legs could see that Kevin was torn between playing with the other kids and staying with Six Legs. "Go on and show them your stuff," he said. "We'll watch from the shade over there."

The portal had reappeared!

Gabloq couldn't keep the joy he was feeling from intertwining with his projected thoughts: *My people must have figured out the new calculations to compensate for the movement of this planet and solar system during the time I've been here.*

Rover picked up on the happiness and added his own. *So, we are leaving?*

For the first time in a long while, Gabloq was at a loss for words. Though he had the ability to hide what he was thinking, he chose to be honest with his companion: *I'm afraid you cannot come with me, my friend. Although our planets are similar, you would not survive the transference through the portal. Our physiologies are very different, and yours is probably incompatible with the technology.*

Rover's panic and dismay were palpable: The dog's body physically shook. *So, what will become of me? We are pack animals. You are my pack. My other pack is gone. Being alone is very difficult for dogs.*

Gabloq hugged Rover with all eight of his limbs. *I will always be part of your pack. My thoughts and memory will always be with you. And you won't need to worry about being alone. I'll make sure of that.*

When Kevin showed up at the park, Six Legs weren't under the redwood tree where they usually met.

Unknown to the boy, Gabloq and Rover were over in the nearby woods, watching as Kevin found the orb tucked among the tree's above-ground roots.

The choice is yours, Kevin, Gabloq thought. *Leave the orb behind and go on with your new life and friends. Or...*

Kevin looked at the orb for a moment, as if weighing both the device and the decision he was about to make. "Four Legs!" the boy called out.

Rover gave his friend from another world one last look of affection and gratitude. Then he burst from the woods with a joyous bark to chase after the orb Kevin had thrown in a long, high arc.

Moments after the dog ran off, Gabloq turned his attention to the glowing portal. Kevin might not be able to project his thoughts or read Rover's mind, but Gabloq was certain their relationship was strong and would grow. After all, Rover had been an alien's best friend.

Now he was Kevin's.

Richard Lau is an award-winning writer who is published in magazines, newspapers, and anthologies, as well as in the high-tech industry and online. His stories have recently appeared in Sci Phi Journal *and* The Last Line Journal. *Two of his stories will be appearing in* Carpe Noctem *(Tyche Books) and* Dark Decades: Capture *(Disturb Ink Books).*

FIDO

BY JENNA HANAN MOORE

OFFICIALLY, MY NAME IS FIDO. I look a lot like an ordinary organic dog, but better. Where organic dogs are fuzzy, slobbery, and dirty, I am sleek, smooth, and clean. Instead of paws, which are virtually useless, I have fully functional hands, and I can walk upright or on all four legs, depending on the task I'm performing.

The name wasn't my idea, nor was my design. My creators thought both would put the organic travelers I assist at ease. Organics are afraid of things they don't understand.

FIDO stands for Faraway Interdimensional Organic, though my full title is Faraway Interdimensional Organic Travel Assistance Bot. I really should be named FIDOTAB, but the only person who calls me that is Rhonda, my organic programmer. She respects me that way.

My job is assisting organics as they travel through interdimensional space to reach new colonies on distant planets. I'm programmed to answer questions, direct passengers about the ship, and read star charts.

Why would organics undertake such a journey, given their fear of the unknown? It's a valid question, but their planet is becoming increasingly inhospitable. Even though organics fear the unknown, they're terrible at caring for things they do know. Like Earth. Rhonda often reminds me that not all organics are fearful or careless. She's right, but organic humans like her are the exception, not the rule.

And organic dogs are worse! From what I've seen, they're stupid, servile creatures, sucking up to humans for approval. They spend their days sleeping, playing, and—worst of all—slobbering. If I must resemble something organics don't fear, couldn't it be something smart, like a dolphin?

"I wish you'd give organic dogs a chance, FIDOTAB," Rhonda said while we were preparing for the next journey.

"I see no reason to like them."

"Dogs can be very helpful." She waited patiently for me to stop laughing before she continued. "I'm serious. Besides, you may find yourself working with a real dog soon."

"That's preposterous, Rhonda."

She sighed. "Lydia Lin, one of the passengers on our next voyage, has a service dog named Rex. Lydia's the lead botanist for the new colony. She needs Rex to help her get around because she's visually impaired."

"Why can't she use a service bot?"

"That's just what she chose. I'm telling you, you'll like Rex if you give him a chance. He's a good dog."

I doubted that very much, but for Rhonda's sake, I promised to try.

On Departure Day, I stood with Rhonda as we greeted the passengers boarding the colony ship. The process took hours. Last to arrive were Lydia Lin and her daughter, Lucy. With them was Rex, a dumb-looking German shepherd who was almost as big as me.

Rhonda shook Lydia's hand. "Welcome aboard, Dr. Lin." She extended a hand to Lucy, who hid behind her mother. "I'm afraid there are no other children her age on this flight."

"We're used to that," Lydia replied. "That's one reason Rex is so important." The shepherd stood motionless at Lydia's side, staring ahead. How important could he be?

"Shall I show you to your quarters?" I asked them. "Or does Rex know the way?"

Rhonda glared at me, but Lydia smiled. "After you, FIDO."

"He prefers to be called FIDOTAB," Rhonda interjected.

"Very well, then," Lydia said. "Show us the way, FI-DOTAB."

I led the Lins to their quarters. Once inside, Lydia removed Rex's harness, and he ran around playing fetch with Lucy. I showed Lydia the climate controls, communications panels, and other features designed to provide comfort. "They operate by voice command once you touch the panels." I looked at Rex. "Err, do you want Rhonda to reprogram them to remove that step?"

"No. Rex or Lucy can guide me to the proper spot, and the panels themselves are brightly colored enough for me to see. But thank you just the same."

"Will that be all?"

"Yes. Thank you."

I nodded and turned to leave, but Lucy tapped my shoulder. "Want to play with Rex?"

"FIDOTAB is part of the ship's crew, Lucy," Lydia reminded her. "I'm sure he has duties to attend to just now."

Lucy persisted. "Maybe you can play when you're off-duty. Like Rex does. He doesn't have any doggie friends to play with on this ship."

"I'm rarely off-duty," I said.

The flight began much like all the previous evacuation flights: The colony ship used the gravity of the moon to accelerate towards Jupiter, then entered the wormhole near Europa that leads into the dimensions we use for travel. There, space curves, and the laws of physics are different, making travel faster than the speed of light possible.

The ride through the wormhole was bumpy. That was normal. Usually, we emerged after an hour and fifty minutes, then enjoyed a smooth flight through interdimensional space for six weeks. After that, we normally flew through another wormhole and emerged in our own dimensions near Terra Nova Alpha. Not this time.

Halfway through the wormhole, the turbulence increased, and the ship accelerated. We emerged forty minutes early in an unfamiliar solar system.

"Link up with the navigation computer, FIDO," directed Captain Martinez. "I've no idea which dimensions we're in, and you're the only one who can scan all the star charts simultaneously."

I did as he asked. "This system matches none of our maps," I reported.

The captain grimaced. "Any way back through the wormhole?"

The navigator shook his head. "Sensors aren't picking up an opening."

"We can't keep nine hundred passengers on this ship indefinitely. Which planets are in the habitable zone?"

The science officer looked at her console. "The fourth and fifth, Sir."

The captain nodded. "Let's have a look at the fourth."

Once we were in orbit around the fourth planet, Captain Martinez announced, "You've got a new job, FIDO. Take Dr. Lin to the surface to scout a site for the colony."

An hour later, I flew the shuttle to the planet with Dr. Lin, Lucy, and a rover. And Rex.

"The atmosphere's almost identical to Earth's," Lydia announced as we made our descent. "A bit less nitrogen and a lot less pollution."

After landing, we stepped out into a lush landscape. The plants looked much like those on Earth, except their leaves ranged from bluish purple to greenish blue. Lydia took readings of the soil while I loaded equipment onto the rover. "The soil's surprisingly rich," she said.

"Does that mean you can set up the colony anywhere?" I asked her.

She shook her head. "It's a bit more complicated than that. We'll need a large enough clearing and an adequate water source. That lake the crew saw from orbit could be perfect, but we'll need enough space near it, and I'll need to test the water."

"What should I look for?"

"Just enough of an opening in the brush that you can see the lake through the trees," she told me.

We boarded the rover and drove east, away from the landing site. Lydia called over her shoulder to Lucy, "I want you to look, too, Lucy, especially off to the side of our path."

"I will, Mama, I promise."

After an hour, we still hadn't found an opening in the dense brush between us and the lake. Lucy had stopped looking. Instead, she snuggled against Rex, stroking his fur. I was right about organic dogs; not only was Rex no help, but he was also hindering our search by distracting Lucy. When we returned to the ship, I'd remind Rhonda that I told her so.

Just then, Rex let out a low growl, followed by a bark. "Stop the rover!" Lucy called. "Rex hears something."

I wasn't about to take orders from a child and an organic dog, but Lydia nodded. "His senses are far better than ours."

My sensors could detect things organic beings couldn't see or hear, not even Rex, but I kept my skepticism to myself and stopped the rover.

Outside, Rex began smelling the ground, walking in an erratic pattern as if following a scent. He stopped, sat up, and sniffed the air, ears erect. Then he let out a long howl, followed by three shrill barks.

Meanwhile, my sensors had detected a sound emanating from the wooded area to our left.

Rex let out another bark and led Lydia in the direction of the sound. Lucy and I followed. Minutes later, an animal appeared in our path, pacing nervously. It had the body of a wild cat, like a leopard or tiger, but it was barely larger than Rex. Its fur was a deep golden orange with black spots, and its tail was long and bushy.

"We'd better not get any closer," I said.

"It's beautiful!" Lucy gasped. "Oh, Mama, I wish you could see it!"

The wild cat wailed. It began walking away from us, then turned around and faced us.

"She wants us to follow her," Lucy said.

"That wouldn't be wise," I cautioned.

Rex whimpered in response to the animal's distress, and Lydia sighed. "I think it's asking for help."

The animal took a few steps away before turning to face us again. When it fell silent, I could just make out the sound of another creature wailing in the distance. Rex must have heard it, too. He tugged gently at the leash and let out another whine. Reluctantly, I told Lydia what I'd heard.

"Then let's follow," she said.

The cat-like creature led us through the brush and down a hill until, eventually, the foliage grew less dense and the hill less steep. Soon, we emerged in a grassy clearing and there it was: the lake! It glittered before us in the sun, its waves gently lapping the shore.

The creature led us to a large tree that had fallen next to the shoreline. Several branches hung out over the water, and others floated on the lake. A few meters beyond the branches, there was an island. Sitting on the island, at the water's edge, was a small animal that looked identical to the cat-like creature. It was crying out for its mother.

"You were right," I told Lydia. "Her baby is on an island. It must have floated there on a branch, or climbed across, but the branch is gone. It's not far, but the tow rope in my tool compartment isn't quite long enough. If we can get the rover down here, we may be able to—"

"Rex can swim!" Lucy called out as Lydia reached down and released the clasp affixing Rex's harness to his leash.

The shepherd ran to the shore, leapt into the water, and swam to the island with a grace even I had to admire. Then, grasping the small animal by the loose skin at the top of its neck, he returned. As he emerged from the lake, he dropped the baby at its mother's front paws and shook the water from his fur.

The mother licked her kitten, who mewed happily as Rex returned to Lydia's side.

"Good boy," she said, patting his head and reattaching his leash.

We watched the reunion for a few minutes. Then we walked along the edge of the lake until we found a large clearing. Lydia asked for an estimate of its size, which I provided.

"It's perfect," she said.

Ten years later, a thriving colony had grown up along the lake. No longer needed as a travel assistant, I've found new ways to be useful. At first, I served as a companion to Lucy and Rex. As Rex grew old and frail, though, I carried him around on my back. Lucy, now a young woman, trained me to be a service bot for Lydia.

When Rex died, we buried him next to the lake, under Lucy's favorite tree. I must admit that I miss him. Rhonda was right about Rex, and I've admitted as much to her.

Never once has she said she told me so.

Jenna Hanan Moore loves to travel, take pictures, drink coffee, and immerse herself in nature or a good story. She lives with her husband and dog, currently in southern Illinois, but she left her heart in the Pacific Northwest. Her tales appear in places like The Lorelei Signal, 365 Tomorrows, Dog Tales, Twenty-two Twenty-eight, Friday Flash Fiction, *and* AI, Robot, *an anthology from JayHenge Publishing. She is the founder and editor of* Androids and Dragons *(androidsanddragons.substack .com).*

Dog Diplomacy

BY E. FLORIAN GLUDOVACZ

"That's disgusting, Lars." Susan sighed and wiped the slimy glob off the main console.

Her friend replied with a goofy grin and a tilt of his head.

"Do you want me to put the collar back on?"

Lars extended his neck and made a low, rumbling sound as Susan affixed the device and sat back in the pilot's chair.

"Thanks," Lars said, his voice now translated and amplified through the collar's speaker.

"Sometimes I really wonder why they gave me a New-foundland as a partner," Susan griped. "This ship is way too small for a giant dog, and it's driving me nuts."

Lars let out a long breath, puffing up his jowls as he considered this. "You know that all courier-class ships require an emotional support animal. Without me, you'd go crazy in no time."

"I'll end up insane either way, but that's not what I meant. Why did the transportation department augment an eighty-kilo breed that sheds incessantly and produces enough drool to fill a bathtub instead of picking a sensible breed like a Pumi? They are small, don't shed, and I can't begin to imagine how much less they slobber."

"Pumis can't carry as much weight as I can, not to mention that my abilities as a water dog are handy in zero-g. I simply swim along."

"I know. We've been through this a hundred times, and I'm not serious."

"I understand. You're bored and frustrated. And you're a terrible neat freak who needs to lighten up." He grinned at her, tongue lolling, then shook his head vigorously, spraying slobber all over the wall and sending a cloud of fur from his undercoat afloat inside the cabin.

"Lars!"

He gave her face an enthusiastic lick, then snuggled against her.

"You're a disgusting fuzzface," she grumbled as she ruffled his ears. "But I love you anyway. You furry monster."

"I love you, too. Now, how about feeding this poor, starving little doggie?"

"You are none of these things," she said with a snort. "But it *is* dinner time, so I suppose I should feed you. On today's menu we have a choice of kibble or different kibble. What'll it be?"

"I think I'll go with the different kibble."

Susan rose and crossed the cabin. She pressed a large, square button at hip-height, and the machine dispensed a portion of dog food into Lars's bowl. "You could do this yourself, you know," she said. "The dispenser was designed for dogs. You simply press the button with your big nose or your paw. So, what gives?"

"It's a dog thing." He ambled over and began munching.

Susan returned to her console to review the day's mission data. Columns of figures were projected into the air in front of her, and the numbers began scrolling in response to minimal flicks of her fingers. Because the processes were calibrated to her preferences, she hardly noticed her own actions, or the machine's responses, as she lost herself in the data. "This is interesting," she murmured under her breath.

Lars looked up from his bowl. "What is?"

"These numbers. If I'm reading this correctly, we might have discovered a Terra-compatible planet in this system."

"That's good, isn't it?"

"You bet your furry butt it's good. In fact, it's more than good. It's pretty freaking spectacular. If I'm correct, we'll have surpassed mission directives and goals. We're supposed to search for resources and minerals, but finding a potentially habitable planet is way better."

Lars licked his chops and crossed the cabin to sit next to Susan. "So, what happens now?" he asked.

"I'll swing this tub around. We'll fly a close pass and see whether the sensor readings confirm my data analysis."

"And then we land, and I claim the planet for New-fiekind? I have the perfect method," he added, lifting one hind leg suggestively.

"Hardly!" she said, laughing. "I don't see any walkies in your immediate future. We'll collect data and return to mission HQ. Perhaps you can have a proper walk after debriefing."

Lars sighed. "Damn bureaucrats."

Susan entered the revised course with a quick flick of her fingers and watched the main display as the planet hove into view. It was a tiny speck, even under magnification, but it would grow in size soon enough. Standard protocols prohibited an approach that would put their little ship into orbit around an unknown celestial body, but they'd get a closer look and collect more data before returning to base.

Every so often, she glanced at the sensor data that scrolled across the projection, but her main focus was the planet on the screen. No amount of data could replace the appeal of the visual experience. And no matter how sophisticated humanity had become, she thought with a wry smile, humans were, on some level, still just fancy monkeys who enjoyed a good view.

"You should eat something," Lars said, interrupting her train of thought.

"I'm too excited."

The Newfoundland turned around and moved to the kitchen area where he nudged a cabinet door open and gently grabbed a nutripack between his lips. After dropping the pack onto his friend's lap, he sat down and stared at her intently.

Susan looked at the nutripak and then at Lars. "So, you can't get your own kibble by pressing a simple button, but you can open a cabinet and pick food for me?"

"Exactly! Now, don't argue. Have a bite to eat."

"It's covered in drool! That's nasty."

Lars rolled his eyes. "Only the outer wrapper, and you aren't going to eat that, so quit debating, and start chewing."

"I guess you're right," she conceded, doing as she was told. "It's just that I've been dreaming of this moment for a long time."

"Eating a packaged meal?"

"No, silly, I'm talking about our discovery. A new planet. It's why I got into this line of work in the first place. I wanted to discover something new! Push the boundary!"

"The final frontier?"

"Something like that. I always wanted to be an explorer, a discoverer, a trailblazer! This is my chance to make history! Not to mention that another habitable planet would be a tremendous asset for humanity."

"Because humanity has been so good at taking care of the ones they already have?" Lars asked dryly.

Susan sighed. "Well, yeah, I see your point. But we are getting better at it."

"I guess you are. Sorry. I didn't mean to rain on your parade. I know it's important to you."

Susan patted the dog's head and turned to finish her meal. "A reality check probably didn't hurt, so never mind."

They sat in companionable silence, watching the planet grow slowly on the display. Suddenly, the quiet idyll was disturbed by a blaring klaxon and a red flashing icon on the screen that made them both sit bolt upright.

"What is it?" Lars asked, alarm coloring his voice.

"A proximity alert, but I don't understand how that's possible." Susan adjusted the sensor settings, glanced at the data, and sighed in frustration. "Oh, damn it!"

"What's going on?"

"See for yourself," she said, switching the display. "It's a spaceship."

"Somebody beat us to the discovery?"

"Not exactly. This isn't a human ship. It's Pangyrian."

He cocked his head, ears perking up. "Pirates?"

"Probably," she said. "But there's only one way to find out." She opened a communications suite, selecting parameters that she hoped would be compatible with the Pangyrians' communications array, before speaking into the camera. "Pangyrian ship! This is human exploratory vessel /Arya/. I am Captain Susan Volovski. We are on a scientific mission. Why are you approaching?"

She ran the message through a translation algorithm and set the comms to transmit. They waited for tense minutes until the computer finally received a return message. She gestured, and the message appeared on the screen.

The face of the Pangyrian commander was a wart-covered mess of blotched browns and grays offset by the spiny crest of quills that lined his neck and forehead. "Human commander," he said, his voice resonating with the crackle of dissonant harmonies at the edge of human hearing. "You have entered the Pangyrian Empire's restricted space. Prepare to be boarded. Your vessel is forfeit, and a message will be dispatched to your command, notifying humanity of this infringement. You and your crew will be terminated."

The message ended abruptly, and Susan moaned. "Oh crap. We're in for it now."

Lars shifted uneasily, his eyes never leaving the alien's frozen visage on the screen. "Can they really do that?"

"Not legally. I'm pretty sure they're freebooters, and I'm absolutely certain this system is unclaimed by any known species. They're just bullying us and rationalizing their way into stealing our ship."

"Can they get away with it?" Lars asked, his tail twitching nervously.

Susan ran a hand through her hair. "Most likely. Look at the size of that ship! It's ten times the size of the /Arya/, and I'm pretty certain they have armament systems that could vaporize us."

"So, what can we do?"

"I'll send another message," she said, clearing her throat before flicking the comms into transmission mode once more. "Pangyrian commander, you have no jurisdiction over this system, and you are committing an act of piracy. Unless you cease your aggression immediately, there will be consequences for you and your ship."

Lars raised an eyebrow at her. "There will?"

"I don't know, but we have no choice. I hope I can bluff them."

After another interval, the return message arrived. The Pangyrian commander's face filled the screen, quills bristling as he spoke. "Human vessel, this is your final warning. Stand down for boarding immediately, or we will take more aggressive measures. You have five minutes to comply and power down your systems."

"He's not buying it," Susan said.

"I wouldn't be so sure," Lars mused, licking his nose thoughtfully. "If they are as powerful as they claim, why don't they simply shoot at us right now?"

"Because they want our ship intact?"

"Maybe, but I don't think that's all there is to it. Can you play their messages back-to-back for me, please?"

Susan frowned. "Why?"

His ears perked forward. "I have a hunch. Play them."

She complied, and the dog watched the alien's countenance with a serious expression on his face.

"Can you run it without the sound?" He studied the commander's gestures and demeanor, then turned to his friend. "Do you trust me?"

"Sure. Why do you ask?"

"I don't have time to explain. Our five minutes are nearly up. I need you to record my reply and send it immediately."

"Your reply?"

"Yes. I think I can get us out of this, but you have to let me do things my way. After all, what do we have to lose?"

"Nothing more than our lives," she said. "But I'm out of ideas, so you do whatever it takes. Go right ahead and speak into the camera. Your collar is patched into the console."

Standing up on his hind legs, Lars rested his enormous paws on the edge of the console. He raised his hackles and released a vicious growl, baring his teeth in a hostile manner while making sure to stare straight at the camera. "Pirates!" he snarled. "This is Lars the Newfie, and you do not want to get on my bad side. We discovered this system, and we're laying claim to it, so you'd better back off unless you're ready for a world of trouble. Leave right now, and never bother us again!" He turned to Susan. "Send it, please."

"Just like that?"

"Yes, do it."

She transmitted the message.

The five-minute mark went by, and then the wait extended to ten tense minutes until the reply arrived.

The Pangyrian appeared deflated, smaller somehow, his warty face framed by quills that were now hanging limp. "Lars. We apologize for the misunderstanding. Let me offer our sincerest regrets. We will withdraw from this system, and we will not return."

Moments later, the pirate ship engaged its engines and moved away from the /Arya/.

Susan was incredulous. "How did you do that?"

"Like I said earlier," Lars replied with a broad canine grin, "it's a dog thing. You paid too much attention to the words and not enough to the body language. The way the commander moved his quills reminded me of a frightened dog: all bark and no bite. If we could have seen the rest of him, I'd bet his tail was tucked." He paused, considering. "Do Pangyrians have tails?"

"I don't know."

"Well, his metaphorical tail was definitely tucked. And my meanest-dog-at-the-park impression did the rest."

Susan gave her friend an enormous hug. "You're amazing, you know that? You saved our lives!"

"I guess I did." He licked her face. "And please tell me how well a Pumi would have handled the situation?"

E. Florian Gludovacz has been a writer, musician, and artist since he was a teenager. Born in Austria, he grew up living in different parts of Europe (Germany, France, the UK, and Austria). He currently resides in rural Southern California with his wife and their mixed Great Pyrenean Mountain Dog.

The P.I. and the E.T.

BY JOHN WEAGLY

THERE WERE SIX OF them, each three feet tall with big eyes, bald heads, and skin the color of a Shamrock Shake. They were wearing black trench coats, and my first thought was *Where did they get those tailored?*

A couple of good photos would show my client what happened and, if I sold them to the right people, would make me a fortune. Cold mud squished around my shoes as I crouched behind a fallen tree with my phone. The fetid stench of dirty water hovered in the air. I was on the bank of the Chicago River and didn't have anywhere to go if one of them spotted me.

So, of course, one of them spotted me.

That morning, a woman in her early-thirties had walked into my office. She was around five-and-a-half feet tall with blonde hair to her shoulders and rings under her eyes that told me she'd been crying more than a person should cry in the middle of the week. I'd been trying to come up with something clever to post on Twitter and failing, so she was a welcome distraction.

"Can I help you?" I asked with my best customer-service smile.

She sat down in one of the chairs facing my desk. "I want to hire you."

"To do what?"

"To find someone." She reached into her pocket, pulled out a phone, and turned it on before handing it to me. Her wallpaper was a photo of a Miniature Pinscher. "Nicodemus."

"You want me to find your dog?"

The woman sniffled and nodded. I could tell speaking would've unleashed a torrent of tears.

"What's your name?"

"Donna," she managed.

"Hi, Donna. I'm Casper. But maybe you knew that because it was painted on the door."

That made her smile a little.

"Why don't you tell me what's going on?"

She took a breath and slowly exhaled. "I live on the Northwest side. Last night, I was walking Nico in LaBagh Woods."

"The forest preserve?"

She nodded. "That's his favorite place to go; there are so many things to stop and sniff. We tend to stay out of the wooded area at night, sticking to the trails, staying on the edge of the trees. Last night, we were walking near where the river cuts through. We heard a weird, whining sound, like a rumbling synthesizer, and a strange, bright glow seemed to surround us. I had a hold of his leash, but he tugged so hard I dropped the handle. He ran into the woods, barking and chasing whatever was making those lights and noises."

The little guy sounded pretty strong for a Min Pin. "And he never came back out?"

"No," she said, sniffling again. "I searched for him, calling his name, waving treats in the air, hoping he could smell them. I gave up after a couple of hours. Today, I called Animal Care and Control and every shelter in the area with no luck. I tried talking to the police, the Park District, and even the Friends of the Chicago River. Once I mention the lights and the weird noise, they treat me like I'm some kind of nut. I want to hire you because, if I pay you, you have to take me seriously."

That wasn't entirely true, since I take very few things seriously, but I didn't want to burst her bubble. "I assume he was wearing a collar," I prompted.

"Yes. And he's chipped."

I didn't have any other cases at the moment, so I took her money with a straight face and told her I'd look into it. Nico probably met a hungry coyote, but who was I to break her heart?

I headed west later that afternoon, taking Foster Avenue to LaBagh Woods. It was a nice little natural oasis in the sprawl of the Windy City with several large, open fields, as well as wooded areas. The north branch of the Chicago River cuts through like the tail of a confused comet.

I entered the visitor center and found a guy sitting at the information desk. He was wearing tan pants and a green polo shirt. He looked like he was happy to be there but didn't want anyone to bother him. His name tag read *Cathcart.*

"Are you a park ranger?" I asked him.

"I'm a volunteer docent."

I would've just said yes. Park ranger sounds cooler than volunteer docent.

"What can I do for you?" he asked.

"Have you seen this dog?" I showed him my phone with the photo of Nicodemus Donna had forwarded to me.

He looked at the picture. "No, can't say that I have."

"He ran into the woods. The owner's worried sick. Do you have cameras around here?"

Cathcart nodded. "We do, but they stopped working last night."

"All of them?"

"There are only a few. They all conked out at the same time. Isn't that weird?"

The cameras going on the fritz the same night the dog disappeared? "Very," I said. I thanked him and went out to wander around the park.

It was cold, November's chill flexing its muscles, and the sun was starting to go down. I roamed around, looking at tree bark and broken blades of grass, pretending I was Daniel Day-Lewis in *Last of the Mohicans.* I had no idea what bark and grass were supposed to tell me. Weird noises filled the air, clicks and buzzes and chirps from insects I couldn't see. I passed under a cement culvert with big-city graffiti on it that read, *I Want To Believe.* After that, I followed the river for a while.

That's when I stumbled across them.

They were busy little space invaders, collecting flora and fauna of every description—leaves, rocks, bugs, tiny frogs, colorful birds snatched right out of the nest, you name it—and putting them in glass cubes of varying sizes.

The one that spotted me gestured for me to come out from hiding, so I did. When I got close enough, I noticed he smelled like swamp gas and sour wine. He tilted his head as he checked me out and then announced, "You should not be here." He didn't have a mouth, but I heard what he said in my brain.

I kept my cool, acting like finding clichés from a Roger Corman movie was an everyday occurrence. "Welcome!" I said. "Where you guys from? Mars? Venus? The Quasar Continuum?"

"You should not be here," the little guy repeated.

Okay, so they didn't want to make friends. "Why not?" I asked, defiant. "This is my planet, isn't it?"

He pointed one of his three fingers. "Go."

"Just a second." I showed him my phone. "Have you seen this dog?"

He looked at the screen. "You call this a 'dog'?"

"Yeah. We earthlings keep them as pets."

His wide eyes grew wider with what I read as alarm. "Pets?"

"Yeah."

He turned his head around backwards and looked at one of his buddies. The other guy nodded and went deeper into the woods. I guess they used more of that telepathy thing. He came out a few seconds later with Nicodemus in one of those glass cubes. He handed it to his boss and went back to foraging.

"We understand pets." He waved a hand over the cube, and it opened. He took Nico out and handed him to me. "We do not want to take pets."

"Thanks!"

He pointed again and said, "Go."

"Where did you get your cool little coats?"

Point. "Go."

"What if I don't want to go?" I asked, feeling a little salty about him bossing me around on my own turf. "You'll disintegrate me with your death ray?"

He looked puzzled. "Would that be unpleasant?"

"Somewhat."

"Then, yes. Go, or we shall death you with our disintegrate ray."

I smirked. "You don't know what a death ray is, do you, you Uranus reject? I bet you don't even *have* a death ray."

He flashed an image into my mind of me being zapped into a pile of bubbles and ash. Nicodemus squirmed in my arms. "We are interstellar beings. We can figure it out."

He made an excellent point. "I should not be here," I said. "I'll go."

My alien friend nodded.

We walked back to my Prius. Nicodemus sat in my lap, making it difficult to manage the steering wheel. I guess, after the night he'd had, he was desperate for contact with humans. Just as I was ready to leave and drive back to my neighborhood, a loud rumble, like someone who didn't know how was trying to play a theremin, rose out of the woods behind us. A few moments later, a bright light shot off into the stars.

We got back to my office, and I called Donna. Even though it was getting late, I figured she'd want her pooch back as soon as possible. I didn't bother writing up a report because what would I say? None of the pictures I took turned out; they were all drowning in static like a TV screen in the 1950's. Without proof, who would believe me?

She was there in twenty minutes. When Nicodemus saw her, he wagged his tail like he was trying to shake it off of his body. Donna cried, and I grew a little misty myself.

I told her to keep a better grip on his leash and encouraged her to watch the skies for stardust wishes and celestial dreams.

She didn't understand that last part, but that was okay.

John Weagly's work has been called "exuberant" by the Chicago Tribune, *"charming" by the* Chicago Reader, *and "appealingly quirky" by the* Chicago Sun-Times. Locus Magazine *once compared his short fiction to the works of Ray Bradbury and Nina Kiriki Hoffman, calling him "a new writer worth reading and following." Over one hundred of his plays have received productions by theaters on four continents. A collection of his short sci-fi/fantasy plays,* Tiny Flights of Fantasy, *has been taught at Columbia College. You can find more of his short stories in the collections* The Undertow of Small Town Dreams *and* Dancing in the Knee-Deep Midnight.

Friends Out of Time

BY ROBERT D. HILL

"TWO LIFEFORMS DETECTED," THE salvagebot spat out in a flat, robotic tone. "Unable to detect species. Please advise to continue operations."

Greyson, the short, silver-haired Minister of Salvage Operations in the Solarite system, sat in disbelief behind his console, watching the camera feed of the bot scouting the remains of the CRS *Hermes*, a syclla carrier left over from the old battles with Gren'Kash.

He was all too aware that sonic drives were unreliable in the early twenty-third century, often failing and sending the ships into a dangerous time-dilation warp. To counter this (and in an effort to keep the crew alive), cryo-genic sleeper pods had been planted on the ships so the crew could wait peacefully for their rescue in interstellar space.

The *Hermes* had not been so lucky, however: A post-battle infection had ravaged the ship, damaging the sonic drive in the process. When crew had tried to refo-cus the drive, it sent them spiraling through time before they could enter their sleeper pods. Now, almost a hun-dred and fifty years later, the *Hermes* had emerged from its time warp, landing in Minister Greyson's jurisdiction.

All that remained of it was the mangled piece of a once-beautiful ship. Scans indicated that ninety-seven percent of the sleeper pods had failed, killing the oc-cupants. Greyson watched as the salvagebot's camera floated above the only two still-functioning pods, both of which were frosted and coated with debris.

"Haul them into the bay so we can inspect them," he ordered, leaning into his microphone. He felt horrible for these poor souls, ripped out of their time and pro-pelled into the future. For them, it wouldn't have felt like a second had passed. Meanwhile, the Reunited Cretian Republic had collapsed and risen twice, and brutal wars had ravaged interstellar borders along with multiple insurrections.

Greyson made his way down to the dull, metal chamber that was the bay. It was illuminated only by the dim, blue lights that lined the rims of the runways plus the reflection of Solarite Prime—the planet they orbited—shining in through the open hangar bay.

The salvagebot, a large metal, mechanical figure that resembled a human but was twice the normal size, had hooked a cable line to the two sleeper pods. All of Greyson's employees fell silent as it gently set them down in an empty area of the bay currently unoccupied by subcraft. Within moments, a sea of neon green and orange vests began to circle the pods.

"Everyone stay back," Greyson shouted. "Don't touch anything." The pods were so ancient that even Greyson wasn't sure he'd be able to operate them. They were solid black hexahedrons, each about eight feet tall and four feet wide. Their glass display screens were coated with a heavy layer of nearly solidified, metallic dust, no doubt from all those decades of the ship being slowly torn apart.

"Larsen, try to open this thing up," Greyson commanded.

In response, a slender man with thick, wavy hair stepped toward one of the pods and started to work out how to use the control panel at its base. "This thing is old," Larsen said. "I'm not sure they're still even gonna be alive when we open it up, Grey." Finally, after he'd toyed with the buttons a bit, a deafening, metallic screech emanated from the pod. The lid stuttered but then slowly creaked open.

The cryoair that had been used to induce sleep when the *Hermes* met with disaster began to seep out, filling the immediate area with a light fog.

"Everyone clear the area," Greyson ordered as Larsen retrieved masks from a nearby rack. "I don't want you all falling asleep!"

Once his mask was in place and he was able to see and think clearly again, Greyson approached the pod, extended the lid to its fully open position, and whisked away the remaining cryoair with his hand. What he saw next caused him to nearly fall backward onto the floor of the bay. "What the hell is that?"

"It's not human, that's for sure," Larsen yelled back. "Is it one of those creatures from Solarite?"

A yelp echoed from within the pod before two white paws emerged, followed by a head, another set of legs, and a tail. Leaping from the pod, the creature bounded onto the ground by Greyson's feet as the Minister of Salvage Operations scuttled backward to avoid contact, not taking his eyes off of it. It was furry and small, about the length of Greyson's forearm, with long earflaps and a scrunched-up, black snout. Its coat was spotted with large patches of white and brown, and its eyes looked almost human.

"Grey, get away," Larsen said, his curiosity now turning to confusion. "I got no clue what that thing is. It doesn't look harmful, but we have no idea what sort of bacteria it may be harboring."

Greyson backed further away from the creature as it began circling the second, unopened sleeper pod. "What would an RCR ship be doing with an alien species?" he murmured to himself as he made his way to the salvagebot that was still standing by the pods in a dormant state. "Larsen, open up the other pod. Whatever's inside that one might help explain what's going on."

Running a scan on the bot produced varying results, but Greyson was able to narrow it down to two possibilities: The creature was either a Feyold from Solarite, matching the four-leggedness and fur but nothing else, or it was an extinct species that Greyson had to open up some filter options to get through. A dog, specifically of the Saint Bernard breed. Greyson almost ruled it out, as those were supposed to have become extinct in the year 2218.

"It's opening up, watch out," Larsen announced as the second pod released another wave of cryoair. This time, much to the relief of both men, a human male emerged. He was completely bald with green eyes, a trait that had become increasingly rare since the *Hermes* met with disaster. He wore the old camo rags of the RCR before they had switched to suits more appropriate for zero-g environments.

"Where am I?" he asked in a hoarse voice, shielding his eyes from the light.

"You are aboard a repair and salvage vessel of the RCR, soldier," Greyson informed him. "You came out of a time warp, and we were able to save two sleeper pods, yours and the one housing this...thing."

The man's eyes lit up as he looked to where Greyson was pointing.

The furry creature yelped even louder as the man clambered out of the pod and toward his shipmate, struggling to walk because of the long sleep he'd endured.

"Careful, we don't know what that is!" Larsen caught the man before he was able to touch the creature.

"What's wrong?" the man asked with a puzzled look on his face. "He doesn't bite. He's fine." He pushed Larsen out of the way and collapsed onto the floor. Scooping the creature up onto his lap, he ran his hand over its coat as it licked his face in return.

"Is that thing yours?" Larsen asked.

"Yeah," the man replied, coughing and trying to clear his voice simultaneously. "Why? Do you guys not know what a puppy is?"

"A what?" Larsen replied, more confused than before.

Greyson stepped down from the bot, his suspicions confirmed. "A dog," he said, approaching the group. "Specifically, *Canis lupus familiaris*. A species that went extinct nearly a hundred and fifty years ago."

A grave expression washed over the man's face. "Wait. How long has it been?"

Greyson got down on one knee to come face-to-face with the man. "It's the year 2383," he said, hesitantly putting his hand out in front of the dog so it could sniff him.

"Alright, alright," the man said in between heavy breaths, still trying to comprehend the situation. "You said dogs went extinct?"

Greyson ran his hand along the back of the creature. Its fur felt extremely soft, almost comforting. "Yeah, a while ago. Probably right after you left or got sucked into that time warp. According to the salvagebot, there was a virus that targeted their immune systems. It was like the black plague for them."

"So, Barry's the last one, huh?" The man stared down into the eyes of the dog.

"Barry?" Larsen asked.

"It's his name," the man said, swinging the dog up in both arms and holding it in front of his face. Barry, you're about to be a scientific achievement."

Greyson and Larsen exchanged puzzled glances.

"This is the future," the man added. "I was on a team that had guarded cloning tech on Europa for awhile. Surely, that's perfected by now."

Searching the salvagebot's terminal once more, it didn't take Greyson long to find articles about cloning tech that had been defunded because of morality issues, but the research stations on Mars and Europa still had a functioning skeleton crew. "The bot says its possible," he informed the others. "Looks like the largest cloning stations are on Europa."

Larsen smiled as he petted the dog, which had nuzzled its head into his hand. "Is that where we're headed, boss? Salvage-team-turned-rescuers of an extinct species?"

"Well, we're gonna finish up this job then head out," Greyson replied. "I'm sure the higher-ups won't mind when they hear the reason." He turned back towards his crew, which had silently been watching from afar. "Everyone back to work. I want this job finished on double time, and no one goes near our guests. Who knows what kind of germs or bacteria all of you are carrying."

"Larsen, get our guests comfortable in one of the extra bunks, and catch him up on the times."

As the crew scurried about, getting back to their tasks, Larsen began to help the man up. "You need anything else, Grey?" he asked.

The Minister of Salvage Operations shook his head. "No, you all get comfortable. I've got some calls to make to Europa."

Robert D. Hill is an indie author focusing on historical and science flash fiction. Growing up in the Adirondacks mountains was a slow and isolated beginning. To escape the monotony of the area, he wrote stories of other worlds for fun which soon turned into publishing the stories at a young age. Writing short stories and flash fiction has inspired him to write longer novels on the side.

Every Cosmos Has a Ruling Class

BY LAWRENCE DAGSTINE

THE CANINE'S ROBE FLAPPED about him like wings. As his paws and face turned heavenward, a whirlwind unseen, unfelt, and unheard, lifted him and his chosen. Upward they fled until they were lost among cold constellations. The balefire flared from its coals, threw spark and flame, and sank again. The pups of the Scooby Luna shuddered and departed, bearing a heavy load of kibble. ..and one unwanted passenger.

Butler wondered, chillingly, how many hounds there were that day. This was a journey not to be underestimated, and no one could oversee every part of space and time. The first ray from the penultimate sun lanced the black belly of a cloud, splashing blood across the soon-to-be Old World.

And yet, the death of a world is only the beginning, Butler thought. He looked up and realized things were merely being postponed. *The ultimate disappearance of stars cannot be prevented,* he told himself. *When the universe is a hundred billion years old, the last generation of stars will be extinguished forever. Darkness will dominate everywhere, and a different cosmos will rule by the gravity that holds dead stars and black holes in its grip.*

That same gravity, once responsible for the formation of clusters, galaxies, suns, and planets, had caused the tragic decline of the humans' hierarchical structure and shaping of the cosmos. So, Butler turned to the heavens. Subtle changes in the motions of planets, small but visible through tiny rips, brought chaos. The gravity of accidentally passing stars tore planets from their orbits and hurled fossilized remains into his wilderness. This slow game of fetch had been going on since creation, and the canines, who possessed a profound sense of intuition, tired of it.

Planetary systems fell apart, stars quit their systems in which they were once born. Galaxies evaporated.

But the evolution of things was not over yet. There was a great recycling going on, and the structure of the cosmos had only just begun. It still had its future ahead of it, though nobody knew when the next Big Bang would occur, or who the next ruling class would be when evolution shuffled its cards. All Butler knew was this: If you no longer focus on the brief events of one, small corner of the universe, but, instead, extend your gaze to astronomical proportions, you can leave the here and now behind, allowing your spirit to gaze into the crystal ball of things to come.

Of all the rigors Butler was forced to undergo, one of the most difficult was the fact that his section leader, Calica, was a cat. Obviously, said leader had been through it all before with the humans, prior to their demise, and she clearly regarded the gasps and struggles of these new canine recruits with easy contempt. Calica was perversely unpleasant and bossy, and she allowed no dog to fail through unfamiliarity or exhaustion (her definition of these two categories only barely distinguished them from stupidity and goldbricking); she was utterly merciless in regard to both.

In response, Butler swore in private, gritted his incisors, and bore down hard. Simple pitbullian pride was not going to allow him to admit that a cat was any better at all of this than he was—the simple fact that she *was* better notwithstanding. Somehow, it quite failed to occur to him that the same thought might exist in the heads of every pooch in the bridge, and that Calica's attitude was expressly designed to provoke nothing else. As for the other mutts in the rafters, shoveling atomic energy cells into their proper cylinders, they were mostly a hardy, uncomplaining, almost offensively cheerful lot, who quickly became frighteningly competent.

At the end of a six-month journey, the section was broken up and reassigned, in groups of two and three, to new and more specialized types of canine training. This still left Butler and Calica stuck firmly together, since he had been so unfortunate as to show talent in piloting and navigation, which was her own area of specialization.

Perhaps the humans of the old ruling class hadn't been so bad, after all.

Though he tried to tell himself that the impression was nonsense, Butler was nevertheless convinced that Calica went out of her way to assign him the roughest, the dirtiest, or the dullest details of every assignment. Since it was impossible to discover a reason for this, he was forced to invent one, this being the instantaneous dislike she seemed to have taken to him when they had first met on Dogonia.

One day, Butler confronted the cat, asking forthrightly, "What makes you think you're so superior to us? You're not even human!"

Calica played dumb. "Whatever do you mean?"

"The way you bark orders. *Dogs* are the next ruling class. It is written in the scriptures. *We* lead next."

The cat licked her paw from the pilot's chair. "Show me."

Butler pulled out a tome. "Right here!" He flipped to a bookmarked chapter. "The recycling process often repeats itself over and over, so a star can grow bigger, and a new breed can lead. The permanent stability of this breed is shrouded in mystery beforehand but determined by a rogue star. The rogue star acts as a beacon and an oracle, in the night sky, of things to come. It becomes the home for the new ruling class. The rogue star swells and shrinks, heaves and puffs, sweats and blows. Soon, large quantities of cool gas that quickly form into fragile molecules—small particles of smoke and soot—are blown into space. In the cosmic blinking of an eye, exhaled mists light up in the most fantastic colors, irradiated by the last surviving star, which is now smaller, whiter, and hotter. Clouds are blown away forever into the dark space between the stars where they become part of a new star, a new source of light and heat, a new phase in cosmic recycling. A new chapter in evolution will rise from the burned-up energy at the farthest reaches of space. This is much faster than the human race evolved into prominence, but the remains of their essences will be the fertilizer to lead interspatial existence anew."

Calica laughed. "And in less time than it takes to melt a scoop of butter over a fire, the stronger side will begin to confuse and dissolve the logic of the weaker side," she said. "That's us. Cats. This will be the moment of war for you. When it is finished, one logic will stand intact, and the victors will install the next phase of evolution...and the next rulers. That's where *we* come into the picture."

"For centuries," Butler countered, "felines have merely existed as temperamental but lazy objects for humans to toy around with. They are animals of behavioral comfort. There was no sharp dichotomy as there was with canines. The humans endured because of *us*. The dogs. We went into battle with them." He smiled. "There is a reason the ancients called us Man's Best Friend. After many millennia, we blended with them, transfigured them, learned to build and pilot their vessels, saw their science triumphant as they had, until furry forms stood upright again and only names and postures had changed. And, always and forever, there were the little puppies, who men brought home to their children, and their children's children, who they made into signs of help and harm, love and fear, every wonderful adoration and fickleness which was life."

"Or it might all be the shadow of some ultimate myth," Calica responded with a shrug. "Dogonia was a shepherd's huddling place, just as Earth was. What mattered in cosmic history was not what men thought of canine companions but what they *felt*. And when it comes to *us*—the cats—we provided the humans with a special kind of affection."

Butler growled. "You do realize that this great, slow conflict and interweaving of two worldviews is why the war between our species has lasted so long, right?"

Calica hissed. "It was purely a question of taste whether humans preferred dogs over cats, and if they chose cats by chance, it made up for all they lacked. The fact remains, the human race was one with earth and sky and sea in a way that those who set the gods apart from themselves, or who denied any gods, could never be. When the humans brought their patriarchal cats to a new planet, they brought much that was good; but with the pantheon that is dogs, they created a new and *lonely* kind of man."

The canine smiled frostily, ending the disagreement with a peculiar writhing gesture of his whole body, as though he had flexed all of his great anomalous muscles at once. His voice, a light tenor astonishing for such a large dog, insisted that Calica prove canines were subordinate to felines to such an extent that the latter should govern and structure the next hierarchy.

"All right," Calica agreed. "Follow me into the bay. I'm going to conduct some research and show you why cats should lead next." She got up from the pilot's chair, produced a large, fragrant bone from a nearby cabinet, and walked to the back of the ship.

They proceeded to the airlock.

Butler couldn't take his eyes off the succulent-looking treat. "What are you going to do with that?"

Calica waved it around. "It's space research, just like I said it would be." She threw it beyond the parameter of the airlock enclosure.

Butler swallowed, unable to take his eyes off the bone. "And it's outright suicidal as far as I can see," he said. "In fact, it's the craziest thing I've ever seen somebody do."

"I don't see any harm in telling you that you're going to give in to pressure and fetch that bone," Calica said.

Butler watched the treat with incredulity; somehow, it spoke to him with a delicate pattern of sound through the portal-like enclosure.

Calica looked amused. "If it's all that suicidal, why are you so hot for it? It doesn't make sense. *This* shouldn't make sense. Not for a species that is next in line to rule the cosmos."

"I suppose not," Butler said, nibbling at one of his paws. "I don't know. What *is* this test, anyhow?"

"You're a pretty sharp animal," Calica said. "I've known that all along. You wouldn't let yourself be entrapped. What's the difference, you ask? That's the kicker."

Butler straightened slowly and looked at Calica as if victorious. He still disliked the feline as much as ever, but he could hardly deny that, in this burst of candor, he found more to admire than he had ever seen in her before.

He realized he had not answered one of Calica's questions as candidly as he might have, though only because he had misunderstood it. Obviously, the purpose of this research had been whether or not he would be able to resist temptation when faced with a predicament aboard an interstellar vessel.

Suffice it to say that, for now, a pitbullian sails through the cold stillness of space, hoping to hitch a ride on a passing ship commandeered by canines, while one tricky little feline makes her way toward a rogue star glowing in the opposite direction.

Lawrence Dagstine is a native New Yorker and speculative fiction writer of close to 30 years. He has placed over 500 short stories in online and print periodicals during that pe-

riod of time. He has been published by houses such as Damnation Books, Steampunk Tales, Wicked Shadow Press, Black Beacon Books, Farthest Star Publishing, Calliope Interactive, and Dark Owl Publishing (with which he has a new book out called The Nightmare Cycle*). Visit him at lawrencedagstine.com.*

On Planet OTS 44

BY SHASHI KADAPA

It was the far, far, imponderable future when Sanskrit, the language of ancients, prevailed. The ancients—obsolete, natural-born humans, or manushya—had gone extinct millions of years ago due to war and environmental changes on planet Prithvi—Earth. Civilization was now controlled by machine algorithms and higher-class, sentient bots. The main objective of these sentient machines was to find new zones in the universe and mine for minerals.

Saramā—a manager-class dogbot—considered the job that lay ahead of her.

Working alongside Devavani the controller, Khanitr the minerbot who checked the equipment, and other helper drilling bots, Saramā probed the environment and scoured the terrain. She used her sensots for this task, special dog-mounted sensors that transmitted data to Devavani, the central server senbot in the transport ship. Their primary mission was to hunt for the elusive, hydrated rock of Dhatu, fill the space pods, and send the samples to their home planet in the constellation Dharwad.

Their secondary objective was to hunt for life forms that could be either subjugated or exterminated; 'life' was, after all, just an obsolete, esoteric term referring to a set of chemical and physical reactions defined by an objective, since all beings were lab-made and carbon-based.

Saramā and her team worked on a desolate rogue planet, OTS 44, a free-floating brown dwarf in the Chameleon constellation near the outer periphery of her home constellation of Dharwad. Saramā's intuition helped her to sense that there was something else on this rock.

Saramā's creators had embedded light-enabled neural network circuits in a chassis and designated her as the manager bot. DNA and RNA, as per the assigned female gender and programmed activity, were impregnated into her assets. With engineered mutation in multiple genes, she could track, sense, attack, protect, and think.

She was called a dogbot, as the ancients had a life form called a "dog" that was a constant companion to manushya. Highly sentient and synced to Devavani, Saramā had four limbs with sensors that allowed her to scurry up hills or climb out of a pit. She could regenerate with a brief exposure to faint starlight, and her chassis and circuits were hardened for the extremely high and low temperatures, pressures, and radiation.

The drillbots hummed and shrieked as they dug deep into the crust.

"Saramā," Devavani asked, "do you detect any life forms?"

"No. There is no evidence anything was ever here."

"What if the life forms are bots like us?"

"Not feasible," Saramā assured her. "My sensors would have detected EMP, changes in temperature, electric and magnetic fields, and other signatures of activity."

Devavani wasn't entirely convinced. "What if the signals bypass you?"

"Then we probably end here."

Billions of years ago, water was trapped in the molecules of what were now, essentially, hydrated rocks on thousands of planets. The team's mission was to send samples for assay and wait for confirmation. If the sample analysis was correct, large mining camps with hundreds of bots would descend and extract the liquid. After they were through, a planet would be reduced to a shell and gradually disintegrate into dust.

After eons of prospecting using an array of tech spectroscopy, density calculation, and differential density models, the onboard system of Devavani had finally detected the water held in hydrated rocks on Dhatu, which meant that this planet would play a key role in generating power for cities and preparing the Amrita that flowed in the chassis of all assets, providing them with power.

"Devavani," Saramā pinged, "my sensots map a deep cave as a possible source of hydrated rocks. Should I explore?"

"With caution."

Saramā and Khanitr approached the cave mouth and looked inside. The faint starlight did not enter the cave. She asked Khanitr to bounce lasers off the interior walls to create a visual map that could b relayed to Devavani in real time.

Saramā very cautiously moved ahead, sniffing to catch any movement. Then, her paw broke a weak, electrostatic barrier. It was an alarm to detect a presence, a transgression, but not to maim the intruder.

A strong burst of static cut off the link, but it was quickly restored.

Devavani's voice crackled across the infrared wave transponder that operated at 50 terahertz and maintained signal fidelity across space and time: "Saramā, what happened?"

"I broke an electron barrier."

"There is an intruder at port 21," Devavani warned. "It's a hacker. Connection requests are flooding my network. Do you sense anything?"

Saramā glanced around. "No. Just a ping of nanoseconds."

"That ping tried to scan your system, then jumped on our data pathway and connected to me. The signal protocol was deployed millions of years ago."

Saramā was momentarily taken aback. "During the time of ancients?"

"Yes, and it may be much older, but my archive databases do not extend that far back. I wrote algorithms to block the attack."

"Devavani, I sense a massive liquid body in a crater. My probe lasers cannot reach the bottom. The other end is very deep, and the bank is very far."

"Is it H2O?"

"Cannot detect any linked H and O elements held in a reaction."

There was a brief pause on Devavani's end of the signal. Then: "Send a drop of the liquid?"

Saramā moved to the edge of the crater and peered inside. Her laser sensors scanned the vast liquid body for signs of life, but there were none. Khanitr lowered a sampling probe and extracted a few drops.

The liquid was transferred to a capsule sent on a courier bot to Devavani for analysis. Saramā surveyed the sheer walls of glass—walls that had formed from massive eruptions billions of years ago—before sending high-res 5D scans back to Devavani. The open ceiling of rocks in this spot allowed in just enough dim starlight to subtly illuminate the floor of the cave and the water below.

She sensed movement.

Without warning, a force seized them, propelling them into the crater.

Saramā and Khanitr countered, firing reverse autojets as they hovered above the expanse of fluid. She sensed the floor rising as a luminescent mist appeared, faintly at first, illuminating the cave further. Drops fell on their chassis as billions of light particles flashed.

"Devavani," Saramā alerted, "the floor is moving, though my sensors show no signs of life."

The response was unequivocal: "Get out of the cave immediately. If you or Khanitr are trapped, all your data, maps, chats, and history will be reverse scanned, leading to our home planet."

The cave was alive now, the walls glowing with luminescence. Switching the jet into scramble mode, Saramā and

Khanitr fled back to the ship, knowing a deep cleaning would be required to remove contamination. Once they'd returned, Khanitr—who relied on the onboard resuscitating systems rather than Amrita for power—crawled inside his recharging pod, connected to the power replenishing unit, and went dormant.

Devavani trawled through all the databases, gleaning data from the far reaches of ancient archives, until the effort made her glow red.

"What info did you find?" Saramā asked.

"The droplet you sent is part of a shadow lifesphere. I think the crater is an incubating cradle where these life forms evolve. The drop has extremely complex structures with pathways that are different from the carbon structures we know. The molecules have differing chirality, meaning they cannot be superimposed as a mirror image. I used all combinations, translations, and rotations. The molecules also have different acid-based structures, with hydrogen cations and OH anions that undergo dipole-dipole interactions."

The dogbot paused briefly to absorb this information. "What is the liquid matter?"

"It's a slurry of liquid ammonia, methane, silica, nitrogen, and xeno nucleic acids held as solid solutions."

"What?"

Devavani continued, "Saramā, these XNAs are alien and defy analysis, since we use carbon-based DNA and RNA. The DNA and RNA in the molecules are replaced by other chemical bonds and structures, giving them non-carbon life forms. These molecules can replicate, consume weaker ones, and clone. They retain memories of their activities, learn, and pass them to their clones."

Bewildered, Saramā asked, "What does this mean?"

"It means they are intelligent, non-carbon life forms."

Saramā still seemed unable to comprehend. "In the cave, we saw luminescence on the floor and walls. We also saw a liquid body."

"Yes, you did. It's possible they want to communicate with you. Then again, they might want to consume you, or harvest your data. We do not have a precedent for such encounters."

"Are they hostile?"

"The drops exude chemicals that trap other molecules," Devavani replied. "I found traces of space dust and rocks in the drop. Minerals are extracted from the dust to gain power."

Saramā remained puzzled. "But the luminescence stopped at the cave entrance and did not come out."

"The cave entrance is probably a boundary layer and a barrier against radiation. The molecules would not survive the radiation outside. Unless they mutate."

"Devavani, I also saw that the walls of the cave were smooth and glass-like, though eroded. They look like the pod chutes from which spaceships are launched, or maybe they're volcano lava tubes?"

"There is clearly a singular purpose for the crater and the plasma," Devavani explained calmly. "I think life began when these molecules were ejected into space by the volcanoes. The molecules latched on to a passing meteor or comet and were deposited on Earth and other places. They reacted to external stimuli and evolved into different forms and functions."

Saramā paused to consider this theory. "The molecules did not degrade when exposed to deep space radiation?"

"I isolated a molecule and exposed it to the internal environment of the ship. Instantly, an impermeable, protective sheath was formed. The luminescence molecule stopped at the cave entrance and did not follow you. If they had come outside, they would have grown a sheath and become dormant."

"What about the hydrated rocks?"

"It requires investigation. The compound $H2O$ is probably a by-product of the molecule reaction and emitted as waste."

"Devavani, I tripped an electronic barrier when I approached the crater. Then, something tried to hack our network."

"It triggered a molecular colony at the entrance, and they warned the colony in the crater of an alien presence. I booted out the illegal connection requests."

"You mean this colony communicates?"

"Yes, through chemical radioactive reactions that traverse at different band widths. I think," Devavani continued, "that this place is what used to be known as the Cradle of Life."

Saramā was incredulous. "What? Life begins here? But then, who placed it here? I do know the ancients spoke of gods..."

"I think we are products of chemical reactions," Devavani offered. "Perhaps, billions of years ago, life on Earth originated from this spot."

"What do we do now?"

"Saramā, recall the drill bots, and we will leave. If we tell our command, then they will destroy this planet like they have others. These molecules will become bots like us to do their bidding. They will be cultivated in labs, and our creators will have endless sources of $H2O$ and life. Whatever force created these molecules wants them to be free and natural."

"You sure?"

"Yes. Our creators are suicidal maniacs and not logical. They killed each other and destroyed Earth. Now, they use us to hunt the universe to find pristine resources they can destroy."

"The ancients had a term for this," Saramā said as realization dawned.

"Gluttonous, edacious, insatiable greed that destroys everything. We bots are created in the likeness of the ancients."

"You're referring to the deep memories in our systems."

"I will purge all traces of our encounter," Devavani informed her. "Your role algorithms and functionality will remain intact."

"But I am a dogbot," Saramā said firmly. "My code demands that I have to guard assets and serve my master."

"Saramā, you *will* be managing and preserving assets and serving our masters. You are not violating any ethics. You are doing what is appropriate. We will take off."

"What if the command finds out?"

"In that case," Devavani responded, "like all other bots, you and I are expendable and will be recycled. Our 'lives' are a small price to pay to save the legacy of the universe. We can either autodestruct now, or we can erase and live to possibly save other ecosystems."

After another long moment of silence, Saramā agreed. "Erase and purge my system, then. We will make saving the universe our mission."

Devavani fired the take-off systems, and the craft departed.

Turning to look at the asteroid one last time, Saramā imagined a green mist bowing in a namaskar, the form of thanks practiced by the ancients.

Based in Pune India, Shashi Kadapa is the managing editor of ActiveMuse, *a journal of literature. An engineer/MBA, his stories across multiple genres have been published in more than 45 US and UK anthologies. Winner of the IHRAF, NY short story prize, he has been nominated thrice for the Pushcart award. Visit him at ActiveMuse.org.*

MYSTERY,
SUSPENSE,
SPOOKY &
PARANORMAL

Blackie

BY R.C. CAPASSO

OCTOBER 2

Things have been pretty bleak lately. Last week, our neighbor across the way, Jane Wilcox, died alone in her house from a fall down the stairs. I was the one who found her while going over to return a pie plate.

Yes, Jane was seventy years old, but she had seemed in good shape. She was out every day, working in her garden and walking along the lanes with her dog Blackie. Jane's brain was sharp, and I never saw her look faint or dizzy. Not once.

Still, life surprises you, and not always in a good way. We'll miss Jane and her quiet friendliness. The worst of it is that Blackie seems to have sickened with grief and strange obsessions.

Goodness, even nature has turned dark. My husband Paul, walking around on Jane's property to see what needed to be cared for, found a fox lying dead. And crows, even a buzzard, fell out of the sky over the town.

If I believed in curses, I'd stay clear of Jane's land. But I have no superstitions. I just call it a low, sad, puzzling time.

Blackie concerns me most of all. He's always been a good dog, friendly and not given to barking or any misbehavior. You could let a child or any other dog near him, and he'd be on his best manners. A border collie, he must be seven or eight years old now. Jane always kept him well groomed, and they seemed to be aging together nicely. I've known human couples that haven't got along so well.

After Jane passed, Blackie just moped around the property. I tried to bring him across to our place, but he couldn't settle down. The sheriff brought over his dishes, a blanket and some old toys (I wasn't ready to go back into that house, thinking of Jane at the foot of the stairs).

Blackie must have been grieving something terrible, because he kept shivering and retching. Fighting to keep even water down.

We let him come to the funeral, at least to the time in the cemetery. He lay quietly through the final words, his head sunk on his front paws. Never let out a whine or a howl. When the coffin was lowered, he closed his eyes like a human who understood. And he came home with me, making no fuss.

I made him a place in the shed, snug and warm. He'll be a good old companion once his grieving is done. For now, he spends the day lying at the edge of our property, head pointed toward Jane's place.

Oct. 12

Yesterday, Jane's nephew moved into her house. I'd hoped to see some life in the old place, maybe children who would play in the yard or a woman who'd care for the flowers. But Jacob Wilcox seems a solitary sort.

Paul has spoken to him, just to say he'd taken the liberty of pulling some of the weeds in the vegetable garden, and Jacob never even thanked him. I gave him my usual pie as a welcome to the community, but we barely spoke five words. Jacob looks a little like Jane, with the same high forehead and prominent nose, but I don't see much similarity in their manners or behavior.

It will be a loss, having that house change from a friendly spot to an unwelcoming stranger's abode. But it's none of my business.

I took Blackie over, of course, as soon as my hands were free of the pie. It's Blackie's home, after all, and in a sense, his family. I'd never meant to keep the dog permanently and hurried to explain this. "We didn't know Jane had any family, and we didn't know who might come to live in the house. So, we just took him across the way. He's been a little sad, I think, and a little sick. But he's starting to eat again..."

Jacob wouldn't even let me finish. He stood in the doorway, the screen door between us, so I could hardly read his expression. But his words made his meaning clear. "Keep the animal. Or kill it. I don't care."

In that moment, I was able to control myself and hold my tongue. But I will never speak another word to such a heartless person. If I see him in the street, I will only nod if I must.

Oct. 13

Blackie seems to both understand and not understand. No matter what I do, each day he goes to the edge of our property and stares across the lane at Jane's house. He does not cross the lane. He makes no sound. He settles on the grass, head pointed across the way, motionless as the Sphinx. He does not flinch at wagons or passers-by.

At night, he comes to me, eats the mush of boiled meat and vegetables I fix for him—poor thing, it turns out that his teeth are weak and old—and he sleeps in the house. A shed is not appropriate for a soul who has endured the losses Blackie has endured, and Paul agrees.

Oct. 17

Blackie has become a subject of talk in our community. His vigil at the roadside attracts attention. And now he has become known for weekly visits into town. He goes each Saturday afternoon, padding silently and at a distance behind the hurrying figure of Jacob Wilcox. This amazes me, because I do not see Jacob as someone who could inspire affection in human or beast. But perhaps I am prejudiced. Perhaps his forehead, his nose, or his scent reminds Blackie of his lost Jane.

Jacob has vehemently complained about the dog's shadowing. To me, to the sheriff. To the shopkeepers, when Blackie stands on the walkways outside their shops and waits for Jacob to emerge. But "there is no law about a dog in the street," the sheriff quite rightly said.

"He should be put down." Jacob's voice cut like a wire; I heard him myself.

"Why?" At least three people asked at once.

"He...he smells."

There was some laughter, and a man who works on a farm just outside town said no one better come sniffing too hard in these parts.

"Well, how do we know he isn't responsible for my aunt's death? He probably got underfoot on the stairs, and she tripped over him. He's always in the way."

Jacob has made no friends in town. Fortunately, no one is foolish enough to blame the poor old dog for anything. The sheriff just turned away in disgust.

Meanwhile, Blackie keeps his distance, padding silently behind Mr. Jacob Wilcox. Lots of eyes watch out to be sure the old collie gets home all right.

Doc, who has only worked on people up till now, promises to have a look at the aging fellow's teeth. He claims he'll enjoy a patient who doesn't have hare-brained ideas about his own treatment.

Oct. 25

Yesterday, I found a piece of meat by the road. Pretty fresh. The ants had barely found it. But it looked wrong. I wrapped it in paper and took it to the sheriff. He smelled it and said he'd keep it.

I went back and shoveled dirt all over the spot, till nothing was left of blood or smell. Then I washed my hands thoroughly.

Blackie sat at the far end of the yard. And we both stared at Jane's house.

Oct. 26

This evening, the sheriff came by, with a deputy standing behind him. He said he'd caught a rat for an experiment, and it died after a small supper of that meat.

He stepped to the road, patted Blackie, and then he and his deputy crossed over to Jane's house.

I heard a high voice, crying out. It could only be Jacob. In a bit, he emerged, white and shaking, with the deputy gripping one arm.

Oct. 28

It all came out pretty quickly. Jacob admitted to killing his aunt, pushing her down the stairs. His trial is set for early next year. Apparently, he wanted to claim the house and the money Jane had set aside. It seems she had a tidy amount, since she always lived so simply and didn't spend much of anything.

Blackie wasn't supposed to bear witness to the figure slipping in by the back door. He was supposed to eat the poisoned meat, the stuff that killed the fox and the carrion feeders. But his old teeth just weren't up to it. He only took in enough to turn his stomach.

Our old boy is doing better now. The doctor removed one tooth and got his gums all cleared up. I cook his meat and vegetables well, and his appetite is back. We'll still have some good years together. I'm the one who walks him now, and he's shown me his favorite spots. I've met some people I'd only seen from a distance in town. People who know how to appreciate a dog.

Just last week, a new family moved into the house across the road. I can't call it Jane's house any more. I call it the Anderson home and know all the children by name, along with their favorite cookies.

Blackie ambles across the road to play with them. Their voices go high with delight when they see him. But when they wear him out, he comes back to us.

He's a comfort, and I think Jane would be pleased.

R.C. Capasso loves stories of hope and imagination in a variety of genres, from ghost and horror stories to mystery, science fiction, and even a little romance. R. C. has published in Bewildering Stories, Literally Stories, Zooscape, Teleport Magazine, Spaceports and Spidersilk, Fiction on the Web, *and* The Last Girl's Club. *Stories have appeared in online and print anthologies including* Red Cape's A to Z Horror *and* The Librarian Reshelved *for Air and Nothingness Press.*

The Lucky Lady

BY WENDY EIBEN

SYDNI TOWERED OVER THE four-pound mutt, waiting for the scraggly little ball of fur to do her business.

She had a soft spot for Roxie who, at twelve, was toothless and nearly blind. What the terrier lacked in vision and dental care, though, she made up for in spunk; some of her favorite activities were lunging at leaves blowing along the sidewalk and unleashing furious verbal assaults at every flower, weed, and pebble she encountered.

Sydni had an even bigger soft spot for Roxie's owner. At eighty, Maxine was still spry enough to be doing the dog walking herself, but her social schedule made that impossible.

This was Sydni's third week dog walking for her elderly neighbor. Unless she had miscalculated, it was also the third week Maxine had forgotten to pay the agreed-upon ten dollars-per-walk fee.

Three walks per day for twenty-one straight days left Sydni's bank account noticing the oversight, even if Maxine did not.

"Come on, Roxie." Sydni coaxed the dog away from her vicious attack on an unsuspecting dandelion.

Roxie complied, stopping briefly to growl at a garden gnome before trotting happily up the front steps of the house she and Maxine called home.

Stepping inside, Sydni heard an unfamiliar voice. Loud. Threatening. Like Roxie on her best day but, from the sounds of it, belonging to something much larger than the purse pooch cowering at her feet.

"Pay up, old lady, or you'll be sorry."

Sydni scooped up the terrified terrier and ducked out of sight just as a bald, burly man in an expensive Italian suit escorted Maxine out the front door.

Roxie's aggressive demeanor had disappeared, replaced with that of a frightened little dog.

Almost as frightened as Sydni.

She carried the trembling canine to the front window and watched as the man put Maxine into the back seat of a silver SUV. Then, she grabbed her cell phone and car keys from the entryway table. She reached down and scooped up Roxie, plopping her into one of Maxine's tote bags before barreling down the front steps and jumping into her rusty hatchback.

She tossed her phone on the passenger seat and then placed the bag containing Roxie gently on top. Sydni turned the key, but the car gave nothing in response.

"Please, not today!" She tried again. Nothing. She looked up to see the SUV turning right at a stop sign down the street. "Come on," Sydni coaxed, patting the dashboard affectionately. She bit her lip and turned the key. The engine sputtered, then roared to life. Sydni threw the car into gear and peeled away from the curb before skidding around the corner after the SUV. "Idiot! I should call the police." She looked at the ball of fur sitting on top of her cell phone, then reached for the phone, drawing a nip from Roxie.

When the light ahead turned red without warning, she instinctively braced the small dog with her hand. Slamming on the brakes, she looked on in horror as her phone slid out from under Roxie, bounced off the floor mat, and disappeared under the seat. She could see the SUV growing smaller in the distance. She glanced right, then left. Finding a break in the traffic, Sydni gunned it. "Hold on!"

Roxie complied, or at least managed to not fly off the seat as the hatchback lurched forward and through the intersection with Sydni ignoring both the red light and the profanities of the drivers with the right of way.

When they reached the other side, the SUV was nowhere in sight. "We lost them."

In response, Roxie dug her snoot into the tote bag and emerged with a small piece of paper clutched in her gums.

Sydni extracted the drool-coated scrap, revealing the logo of The Lucky Lady Casino. "Here goes nothing."

A few minutes later, she pulled to a stop in the Casino parking lot and looked down at Roxie. "Should you stay here? Keep an eye on the car?"

Roxie let off a series of high-pitched barks.

"Alright, then," Sydni said to the pooch nestled in the tote bag. "But keep quiet. There's no way you're passing for a guide dog." She eased the squirming bag over her shoulder and made her way toward the door.

Once inside, they were assaulted by the sound of constant bells and whistles from hundreds of slot machines, each occupied by a white-haired senior citizen. If Maxine was here, it was going to be like finding a silver-haired needle in a sea of silver-haired needles.

Sydni cursed under her breath.

The bag over her shoulder started to wriggle and growl. Then, Sydni saw them. The large man had Maxine's arm firmly in his grip.

She sprinted in their direction, weaving through the long rows of flashing machines. "Maxine!"

Her voice was drowned out by the shrieks of an elderly man and the blare of an alarm as his 'spin' yielded the hourly jackpot. Suddenly, all of the octogenarians were in motion. They swarmed the winner with a slow, shuffling, flash mob celebration.

Sydni found herself caught in the sluggish flow. She watched as an elevator door across the room opened then closed with Maxine on the other side. Breaking free of the mob, she made her way to the elevator. As she reached for the button, a large hand grabbed her wrist. Sydni found herself face-to-face with two very imposing security guards.

"Sorry, Miss. Private elevator."

She looked past the burly men to the sign listing the elevator's only destination: the penthouse.

Roxie let out a grumble. When the guards looked quizzically at Sydni, she grinned and patted her stomach. "Which way to the buffet?"

The larger of the two men, sporting a bleached Mohawk that rapidly changed colors in response to the flashing lights of the room, pointed to a bank of elevators at the opposite side of the room. "Up to six—and try the crab cakes. I hear they're especially good today."

The other man nodded in agreement as Sydni hurried back across the room. She had waited on her fair share of tables over the years, and there were two things she knew for certain: the kitchen was always near the buffet, and you could always reach the penthouse from the kitchen.

Exiting on the sixth floor, she found herself in line for the early bird special. The crowd engulfed her, knocking the bag from her shoulder.

In the blink of an eye, Roxie was on the loose.

The small dog ran under the stanchion separating the waiting diners from the food being carried out and placed on the buffet. Sydni dropped to her knees to follow when a massive hand reached down and pulled her up by the seat of her pants.

"You again!"

For a second time, Sydni found herself face-to-face with the security guard and his bleach-blond Mohawk. A scream from inside the restaurant, followed by a loud crash, startled them both, and he released his grip.

Crash after crash followed. The guard jumped the stanchion with Sydni close on his heels. Turning the corner, they found Roxie surrounded by the carnage of what had been the early bird buffet.

"Roxie!" Sydni rushed toward the furry rascal.

The security guard cut her off and lunged for the troublemaking canine but lost his footing on what was once the day's pasta special. As he went down in a heap, Sydni scooped up Roxie and deposited her back into the tote bag.

The kitchen emptied of all the servers and cooks as they rushed out to see the commotion.

Sydni pointed at the large man, now covered in marinara. "He did it!"

The guard's face turned as red as the sauce. He tried to get to his feet but slipped again. As the servers attempted to help him up, Sydni ducked into the kitchen and made her way to the service elevator.

There were only two options: "G," which she guessed would take her down. She could hit that button. Maybe forget about Maxine and whatever it was she had gotten herself into.

And then there was "P," which would no doubt take her up. To what exactly, she wasn't certain, but as she peeked into the bag at the tiny dog now covered in a multicolored splatter, she knew she'd come too far to go back.

The elevator doors opened directly into the penthouse.

The large, bald man in the expensive Italian suit who had made off with Maxine earlier was clearly expecting someone, but from the look on his face, it wasn't Sydni. "Who are you?"

The gruffness of his voice startled her and set Roxie off on a barking frenzy. The tote bag shook furiously against

Sydni's side until the seam gave way and the tiny dog fell to the floor.

The man scooped her up. "Roxie?"

"Let her go!" Sydni's voice shook almost as much as her body. She watched as he lifted Roxie to his face and found himself on the receiving end of a barrage of puppylike kisses.

"Wait a minute," Sydni said with a bit more conviction. "You know her?" As she looked on with a puzzled expression, Maxine made her presence known.

"Sydni! What in heaven's name are you doing here?" Maxine collected Roxie from her bodyguard's grasp, rescuing him from the overly affectionate pooch. "Mario, this is the dog walker I was telling you about." She elbowed him in the ribs. "She's single, you know."

Mario tried to look at Sydni but felt his cheeks grow hot and his throat get dry. Usually the most confident man in any room, he found himself blushing too much to make eye contact.

"My goodness, Sydni," Maxine said. "Please come in. I'm a bit confused as to why you are here and, for that matter, how you found me. No one knows I own the place, or at least I don't make it public knowledge."

The elevator doors opened again, startling Sydni. The sauce-covered security guard stepped out leading three well-dressed, elderly women. He locked eyes with Sydni and mumbled through gritted teeth, "The ladies are here for bridge."

Mario regained his composure and stepped forward, blocking the path of one of the women. He reached his hand toward her. "You got my message?"

The lady reached into her bra and pulled out a somewhat damp five-dollar bill.

"I forgot my buy-in one time," she huffed, handing him the five-spot. "You know I'm good for it."

Mario shrugged. "Sorry, Mom. Just doing my job."

She reached up and pinched his cheek. "You're the best strong arm on the block."

He blushed again and looked away, clearly trying to hide his red cheeks from Sydni. "Here you go, Aunt Max." He handed the money over to Maxine who slipped it into her pocket before turning her attention back to the dog walker. "Sydni dear, why are you here?"

Sydni looked around the room, noting the elaborate furnishings and the elegant spread prepared for the afternoon's guests. Realizing that Maxine was not hurting for cash and that now was as good a time as any, she took a deep breath. "I came for the money you owe me." She smiled. It felt as if a giant weight had been lifted from her shoulders. The smile faded and the weight came crashing back down, however, when she met Mario's stern glance.

He turned that glance to Maxine. "You haven't been paying her?"

It was now Maxine's turn to blush. She was known for being a woman of her word, but she wasn't above conveniently forgetting her debts every now and again if it meant a boost, even a small one, to her own personal bank account. She cleared her throat. "It must have slipped my mind."

Mario shook his head and looked back and forth from his mother to his aunt with an incredulous expression on his face. "You two really are peas in a pod, you know that?" He turned to Sydni. "What does she owe you?"

Sydni gulped. Math had never been her strong suit, and looking at Mario gave her butterflies. "Two-hundred and...ten?" Her voice was shaking again.

Mario pulled out his wallet and counted three, crisp one-hundred-dollar bills. As he handed them to Sydni, his hand brushed hers for a moment longer than necessary, and Sydni felt her own cheeks getting warm. Then, he turned to Maxine. "You owe me now, Aunt Max. I'm sure you won't forget."

Maxine waved him off. "Of course not, dear." She handed Roxie back to Sydni and motioned to her friends. "Come on, ladies. Bridge waits for no one." She took a step toward a waiting card table, then turned back to Sydni. "Dear, I believe it is time for Roxie's walk. Would you be so kind?"

With that, the elevator doors opened, and Sydni stepped inside with Roxie cradled in her arms. When the doors closed, she pressed the button for the ground floor. She looked at the small dog and then at the crisp bills in her hand. "Come on, Roxie," she sighed. "I think this is the beginning of a beautiful friendship."

Wendy Eiben is a Pittsburgh-based screenwriter who is bound and determined to write fiction. If she isn't writing, you will find her with her cat on her lap. If she is writing, you will find her with her cat on her lap.

The Dog in White

BY ANTHONY BOULANGER

OBVIOUSLY, GIVEN MY CURRENT state, I should have been suspicious.

But what can I say? I've always loved animals. I also love mysteries, and this white dog was clearly one of them.

At first, it was just an impression caught out of the corner of my eye, a movement in the rearview mirror that made me frown, a fleeting glimmer that passed for a flash of light, no sooner seen than gone.

Then, as the days passed and I drove along the road, it became clear to me that there was... something. The impression became a mist, the mist a silhouette, and the silhouette a dog. Every time I stopped on the bend to approach it, to try to coax it, it disappeared behind the trunk of a tree, vanishing into a shadow or a gap of light between the roots. There was nothing natural about this appearance, and I felt a chill.

I'd always been fond of supernatural manifestations. As children, my cousins and I had dabbled in spiritualism. Today, everyone is convinced that it was one of us who knocked under the table or pushed the planchette in a certain direction with our fingers during our "séances," but I know that none of us could have invented the name of our interlocutor: Madame Croc de la Taranne. I still have nightmares about it sometimes. But that dog...

There was nothing distinctive about it, apart from its ability to disappear in the blink of an eye and the aura that emanated from its fur. I couldn't determine the breed, though something like a Doberman would be my best guess.

"Hey, you," I called to it one summer evening.

The light of the setting sun enveloped the apparition in a reddish halo. When it straightened up, ready to go, I immediately knelt down, taking care not to look it in the eye, lest this be seen as a sign of aggression.

The apparition (I could see it was female now) took a step back with her tail between her legs, ready to bolt. I sat down in the grass by the side of the road, still soaked from the afternoon shower. The water immediately soaked my pants, but I managed to remain stoic. It wasn't until I was cold and numb and the light was razor-sharp that the ghostly dog made up her mind to approach and sniff me. I knew I was having an extraordinary experience. I could see right through the creature, could feel an icy breath emanating from her body and passing through me.

"I'm not going to hurt you," I said, holding out my hand.

The dog laid her ears flat and slowly retreated, passing backward through the trunk of the nearest tree as if there was nothing there. By the time I got up and walked around it, the animal had disappeared completely. It didn't matter, though. This was only a postponement, and I already had an idea or two to crown my next attempts with success.

A week passed before I saw the dog again. I began to drive past her road and turn several times a day, using the slightest pretext—running errands, getting money from the bank—to give myself a good reason to take the car.

When she finally reappeared, I parked in my usual spot and got out slowly. It was dusk, and the dog's luminous silhouette stood out against the brown and green of the undergrowth.

"Hi," I said. "I brought you a few things today." I gently reached into my pocket as I spoke and pulled out a packet of dog treats.

The creature sat up and tilted her head. She stretched out her muzzle, made a sniffing gesture, and wagged her tail. Picking up the treats at the supermarket, I'd wondered if she still had a sense of smell, but everything suggested she did. Was she even going to be able to enjoy them?

"Shall we go a little further?" I asked in a soft voice as I slowly rose to standing and began to walk. I preferred to stay away from the road when her aura was so visible. Perhaps it was selfish of me, but I certainly didn't want anyone else to get ahold of the white dog.

Whether she understood me or not, she followed in my footsteps, staying a few yards behind as we walked along the path until we reached an open spot among the trees.

As I'd done the last time, I sat down on the ground, roughly in the center of the clearing, and left the dog alone for a moment.

She began by circling the glade—once, twice—her eyes fixed on me before sitting down where I could see her, but too far away for me to reach out and actually touch her.

"Okay, girl. I think we can move on to the next phase." I took a treat out of the packet and held it out in front of me.

The white dog didn't move. She just wagged her tail and yelped. At least, that was the impression she gave, since no sound came out of her mouth.

"I'll give you this one," I told her. "But you'll have to come a little closer for the second." I tossed the treat, which landed near her front paws.

The dog wiggled forward and sort of...soaked up the biscuit. It appeared to become dryer and dryer until it fell into dust and became...part of the dog, I guess. She then proceeded to back into a waiting position. Her light seemed brighter—more *dance-like*—all of a sudden.

Remaining on my knees, I gently tipped forward and placed another treat between us, then another right in front of me, and resumed my place with a final biscuit in my hands.

All around us, night continued to grip the woods, but the light of the white dog easily countered it, bathing the whole clearing in its bluish glow. Somehow, I didn't feel frightened at all. This dog must have had a story before she turned into a spirit; she had manifested herself to me, and it was my duty to help her as best I could, to understand and alleviate her suffering if ever she was in pain.

I suddenly realized that the dog was standing right in front of me. Lost in thought, I hadn't seen her approach and absorb the other biscuits. She was just inches from my hand. Once again, I could feel the icy breath escaping from her nostrils onto my skin, breath so cold that I could no longer feel the tips of my fingers.

With unexpected delicacy, the animal seized a flap of my coat between her white fangs and pulled until I stood up. Then she took several strides towards the forest before stopping and looking back at me.

"I'm coming," I assured her. "Don't worry." And so I followed in the footsteps of the canine specter, heading off into the forest without a backward glance.

Night fell. The glow of the dog guided me through the trees until we finally stopped in front of a hovel that had seen better days in another century. After standing there for several moments, the dog began to enter the dwelling before looking back at me again.

Obediently, I followed, crossing the threshold of the open door. As if on cue, it closed behind me with an eerie thud.

The only room in the house wasn't pitch-black, despite the absence of daylight. Apart from the dog, another source of pale light lay on a straw mattress.

"Come closer," breathed a woman's voice.

I stepped forward and leaned in toward her, stunned but eager to help, to understand this experience, and (if I'm to be honest) to extend this plunge into the paranormal. If the white dog had brought me here, I thought, it was surely because here lay her hope of being delivered from her condition. Perhaps I could also help this woman (to whom the dog was clearly attached).

"Don't you find it insulting," asked the ghostly young woman, "that nobody stops for me anymore on the bends in the dangerous roads? People used to stop, even for strangers. Let alone a woman."

Not knowing whether I should speak or run, I did neither.

"See how weak I am," she continued, "without prey, without sustenance. Now I have to use an animal to arouse a little pity."

My eagerness turned to horror as a skeletal hand seized the front of my shirt before I could step back. The white dog locked its jaws on my ankle, and I watched, wide-eyed and speechless, as the lady in the white wedding dress struggled to her feet. The last thing I saw as a living human was that hand reaching for my eyes, and the last thing I heard was the woman congratulating her dog.

"You're a good girl, my dear Madame de la Taranne," she said.

Born in the Rouen area of France, Anthony Boulanger now lives in the Norman country-side in the company of his muse and their three children. He works on short stories, novels, and scripts for role-playing games and comics in the fantasy and science-fiction genres. His favorite subjects are birds, golems, and world mythologies.

Person Detected, Front Porch

BY CHAD ANCTIL

THE SECURITY CAMERA SETUP was my wife's idea, due to the number of packages she got on a weekly basis and the ever-increasing threat of 'porch pirates' in the neighborhood. It wasn't an expensive setup, just a couple hundred bucks, all connected to the home WiFi, but the cameras had a nice clear picture, and there was a feature to identify what each camera was seeing. We would get little alerts on our phones, such as 'animal detected, backyard' or 'package detected, front porch.'

When we first got the cameras installed, we'd look at the feed whenever we got an alert. Usually, it was nothing—someone walking by, or a squirrel in the backyard. Occasionally, it was something cute, like a bird perched on the camera housing or a bumblebee hovering in front of the lens.

After a while, though, the novelty of the system wore off, and we only checked the feed sporadically. We knew anything in the backyard was just going to be squirrels or birds, or sometimes the random neighborhood cat. Once in a while, we'd catch a chubby raccoon or a skunk looking for a snack, but it was rarely that interesting.

The images from the front porch camera were more diverse, however, capturing neighbors walking by or schoolkids headed to the bus stop down at the corner. Of course, we always knew when the mail was delivered—the system worked great for that—and we never had to worry about getting valuable packages stolen. But what I came to love most about that camera were the images it captured of people walking their dogs.

I have always loved dogs, big and small. We can't have one due to allergies, but I still enjoy watching them at rest or at play. Our neighborhood is a quiet one, and our house is just down the street from a large park, so all day we'd get alerts like 'person detected, front porch' and see someone walking their dog past the house. I checked all the alerts, and I got to know several of the local dogs—if not by name, then at least by sight. There was the playful Golden retriever and his harried owner, who usually paid more attention to her phone than to her pet; the huge Great Dane walking calmly beside her diminutive owner; and the stately German shepherd walking patiently beside an elderly man, sometimes stopping to ensure his owner could keep up.

A pair of yappy Pekingese came by daily, constantly tangling their leashes as they ran to investigate every item of interest. The funniest thing about the Pekingese twins was their walker. He was a large, muscular man who wore denim vests and engineer boots and carried a chain wallet, but he doted affection on those little dogs and some-times just picked them up and kissed them for no reason. 'Dog-cam,' as my wife called it, was a fun daily distraction; I looked forward to sneaking in peeks when I was at work all day just to check in on the dogs.

When my job moved to remote and I was working from home, I set up my workstation in the front room where I had a view out the window onto the porch and the front yard. This was a comfortable space to work uninterrupted, and it had the added advantage of letting me watch the dogs in real time, not just on the security camera app.

Over the ensuing weeks and months, a pattern solidified: As I sat at work, my phone would alert me and I'd see 'person detected, front porch', but instead of opening the camera app, I'd peek out over my monitor to see who it was. If it was a dog walker, I'd just watch them amble by. In nicer weather, for some of them, I might even step out on the porch, giving them a wave and a smile. Sometimes, one of the dogs might even see me and run over, and, with the permission of their owner, I might give them a scratch or a pat between the ears and tell them they were a good dog. It was a small thing, but it grounded me and always made me smile. When I was having a bad day, seeing some of the dogs, especially the Pekingese or the bouncy Golden, would always buoy my spirits.

The security cameras were a decent system, and they were reliable overall, but no software is perfect. Sometimes, it would mis-identify things. An alert for 'person detected, backyard' might pop up for a squirrel, for example. Because of this, it wasn't terribly unusual to see 'person detected, front porch' and not see a person, or see 'animal detected, front porch' and see a car driving by when I peeked over my monitor to check. That's why I didn't think anything of it when I saw 'person detected, front porch' and saw only a familiar German shepherd walking himself calmly down the street toward the park.

Unleashed dogs weren't that common in the neighborhood, but they weren't unheard of, either; the local leash laws weren't really enforced. As long as a dog was well-behaved and didn't chase people, they were mostly left to complete whatever doggy mission or exploration they might be on. I recognized the shepherd, of course; his name was Odin and he belonged to an elderly man, Arthur, who lived one street over. The shepherd was an older dog and always well-behaved. I imagined his owner might not be able to take him for his walk to the park, so Odin was just tracing the familiar, well-worn path on his own.

The third or fourth time I saw 'person detected, front porch' followed by Odin walking himself calmly down the street, it was a gray day, and the clouds were threatening rain—I could feel it in the air. I stepped out onto the porch and called out to the dog. He turned to look at me, seeming confused, then turned to look behind him, and then back at me. He walked over to me slowly, and, as he approached, I could see the years reflected in his eyes and on his gray-flecked muzzle. He carried a certain sadness. I petted him calmly as he sat in front of me, all the while talking to him and asking where his owner was. That's when I heard someone else calling him.

A middle-aged woman with a kind face was walking slowly toward us with a red leash in her hand. I remembered it as the leash I'd seen on Odin when his owner walked him.

"Hello, I'm Brian," I said, holding out my hand and standing. "I was just having a chat with Odin here."

"I'm Amanda." She took my hand and nodded, then knelt down to clip the leash onto Odin's collar. "He keeps slipping out," she said with a heavy sigh. "And he always seems to come this way."

"Odin and his owner, Arthur, walk by here pretty much every day on their way down to the park," I told her. "He's probably just missing his walks."

"Arthur was my dad," Amanda said softly. *Was.* Her eyes were puffy, and I could see she carried the same sadness Odin did.

"I'm sorry." I think I said it more to Odin than to the woman who had just lost her father, but she thanked me anyway.

"He went in his sleep. So that's a blessing, I suppose. We all knew it was coming mentally, but...you're never really ready for it emotionally." She shook her head. "Anyway, thank you for looking after Odin. I think this has been as hard on him as it has on anyone."

I nodded in agreement but couldn't think of anything more to say. She started walking back the way she came, pulling on Odin's leash, but the dog didn't seem to want to follow.

"Maybe...maybe try taking him down to the park," I suggested. "His old route."

Amanda shrugged. As soon as she started heading toward the park, though, Odin stood up and fell in beside her, walking just as he had walked with her father, with a bit more wag in his tail.

Why I did what I did next, I can't explain. Maybe it was curiosity, or maybe there was some strange feeling in the back of my head, but when I got back into the house, I opened the security camera app and looked at the most recent feed. There I was, talking to Amanda, and there was Odin, sitting calmly, but then...

It was the video from the initial alert—'person detected, front porch'—and there was Odin, walking down the street. And, amazingly, there was Arthur, or at least some fragment of him, some faded memory that remained, a wispy gray apparition gliding silently beside his loyal dog for one last walk. I stared at it, transparent but solid, undefined but having the same build and pace I had seen a hundred times or more.

I saw myself, in the video, stepping out onto the porch and calling to Odin. I saw his confusion, and then that turn—he turned back, to look up at Arthur, at his lifelong companion. Then, I saw that thin, shadowy figure give a barely perceptible nod 'yes' before the dog walked over to me.

Finally, I checked the part of the feed where Amanda and Odin walked back down toward the park, and tears welled up in my eyes. Maybe it was a sudden break in the clouds, or maybe it was something else, but as the pair walked away, a column of light seemed to bathe them in a warm glow. It followed them down the street until they were around the corner and out of view.

Chad Anctil hails from Rhode Island, the birthplace of H.P. Lovecraft. His fascination with horror began at a young age, perhaps too young. By day, Chad works in cybersecurity, but when the candlelight flickers, he writes. His bestselling debut novel, The Midnight Tree, *explores a supernatural mystery with a nine-year-old boy and the ghost of the young girl haunting his bedroom. His upcoming urban fantasy crime series,* Providence SCU, *follows a secret team of police who fight supernatural crime and dark magical forces in Providence, Rhode Island. Additionally, his horror, crime, and weird fiction short stories have found homes in various anthologies, including* Christmas of the Dead: Yule Cat Codex, Flash of the Dead: Requiem, Masks of Sanity, Halloweenthology: Jack O' Lantern, Apocalyptales, *and* Dead Girls Walking, *among others. He also posts stories and thoughts on writing on ChadAnctil. com*

A Breakup in Three Acts

BY SUE WALSH

I. Teddy

Lauren hated appointments in this building. All the hallways and staircases were on the outside, like an old motel. Looking down through the open risers was giving her vertigo. Without warning, a little white dog came flying around the corner at the far end of the long, second floor hall. It was followed by a frantic young man and woman, who were lagging well behind. Lauren dropped her bag and laptop case and crouched down. If the dog got past her, it would hurtle straight down the steps and out into a busy parking lot.

Lauren needn't have worried. When the dog reached her, it launched itself into her arms before dropping onto its back to wriggle and beg for belly rubs.

Lauren obliged. "Hey, little girl, where you going in such a hurry?" she cooed at the pup as the young couple caught up.

"Who the hell are you?" the man demanded, "and how do you know our dog?"

Wait. *What?* This wasn't the reaction Lauren expected.

She straightened as the guy reached down and roughly grabbed the dog, his face contorted in anger. "How do you know this dog?" he demanded again.

"I...I don't, "Lauren stammered, bewildered.

"You must know her," the girl chimed in. "Do you work at a vet office?"

"No. No I don't. I'm—"

"Are you sure?"

Am I sure?! Lauren thought. "I'm a private investigator. I have my own firm."

The girl looked unconvinced. "You never worked for a vet? Or at a groomer? In the back where we wouldn't have seen you?"

Lauren got quiet as the interrogation continued.

"You must know her," the guy insisted. "Teddy isn't friendly. She never goes to anybody."

Lauren raised her hands in a gesture that was part shrug and part surrender. "I don't know what to tell you. I've never met your dog. Funny thing, though. When I was a little girl, I had a Westie who looked just like—"

"Stay the hell away from this dog," the guy spat out, interrupting her. With that, the couple turned and walked away, Teddy firmly in the guy's arms.

Lauren bent slowly to pick up her belongings while watching them go. They turned back once, as if to make sure she wasn't following. She marked the hostility on both of their faces...and maybe something else in the girl's eyes?

Well, she thought. *That was really odd.*

II. Sarah

"Teddy's dead, Rob. She's *dead.*" Sarah held the phone away from her ear, anticipating the explosion at Rob's end and grateful he was a plane ride away, at a conference.

There was crashing sound, followed by a torrent of incoherent curses that eventually resolved into "You stupid bitch. What the hell, Sarah? How did you let this happen?"

"Nice, Rob. No 'Poor Teddy.' No 'I'm so sorry, sweetie.' Just go right to blaming me." Sarah spoke in a flat, emotionless tone as Lauren sat close by for moral support, monitoring the conversation. "I didn't want to tell you over the phone," Sarah continued, "but I also didn't want you to hear it the minute you got back tomorrow night." She paused and took a breath, trying to calm her nerves. "I just went out to get an Amazon box off the porch. There was a woman with a big dog across the street. Teddy bolted out—you know how she is. Went right for the woman's ankles. Then the woman's dog...."

She could hear Rob banging his fist and muttering while she spoke. Then, as if she couldn't hear all of that, his tone changed instantly.

"Look, Sarah," he said in that creepy, conciliatory voice she knew all too well. "Of course I'm sorry. But I know Teddy has been a problem. When I get home, maybe this will give us a chance for a fresh start, and—"

"Goodbye, Rob." Sarah disconnected the call and slumped back, letting out a long exhale as she looked at Lauren. "Was I ok? I sounded convincing? Maybe I didn't sound sad enough?"

"You were great," Lauren assured her. "You sounded numb. Maybe a little angry. Which was honest."

Just then, Lauren's business partner, Nate, stepped into the kitchen. "I second that," he added, giving them both a thumbs-up. He'd been in the hallway disconnecting a surveillance camera but heard everything. "Tears and wailing might have sounded phony," he said with a grin, "especially since, you know, Teddy is alive and well."

At his words, Sarah burst into actual tears without warning. It was beginning to sink in that this nightmare was over: She might never even have to talk to Rob again.

"I'm okay," she told Lauren and Nate through the tears as they fussed over her. "Really. I just realized I'm about to put this all behind me." She took a moment to collect herself and then continued, shaking her head. "I still can't believe it. That day we met, when you said you were a private investigator, that you had a little dog like Teddy. It was, I don't know. A sign? I remember feeling a glimmer of hope. I cannot thank you both enough."

Lauren patted her back. "Give yourself credit, Sarah. You were the one who tracked me down in the coffee shop and reached out for help. You worked with Rob. Moved into his condo. Breaking up was going to leave you without a job or a place to live."

"And you had to protect Teddy," Nate said as he looked at the photos of the Westie on the kitchen table, the ones they'd printed out from the surveillance camera they'd installed. The footage had clearly shown Rob picking Teddy up by her collar, hurling her into the hall closet, and slamming the door because she was barking. "You got yourself out. Got Teddy out safe." Nate paused. "As for thanking us, you could pay our bill."

Lauren's mouth gaped open. "Nate! We talked about this," she said firmly as she and Nate both burst out laughing. "Seriously, Sarah. Our services are on the house. It was Nate's idea, and I agree. This was a labor of love for both of us. One of our favorite cases, start to finish."

Sarah smiled as she recalled what Lauren had told her in the coffee shop about her partner, Nate, and his soft spot for dogs. "Still. Thank you. I'll make it up to you some way. When I'm working again."

"So," Lauren said, shifting direction. "Ready to go?"

"Yes. I'm picking up Teddy at my mom's. It was smart leaving her there," Sarah said. "Guess it wouldn't have been good if Teddy started barking while I was telling Rob she was gone."

"Plan's the same?" Nate asked. "You're heading down to the beach to stay with your cousin?"

"For about a month. Just to decompress. I can start job and apartment hunting online from there."

"So, you still think you'll be coming back here?"

"I want to," Sarah answered. "You really think it's safe?"

"I do. Rob has no history of stalking his exes. Once he gets dumped, he rewrites history so that nothing is his fault, and they aren't worth the trouble. Teddy was a different story. She could have been a target. But as far as Rob knows, Teddy's dead."

Sarah nodded, grateful for the reassurance. "I'll meet you out at the car," she said getting up. "Give me a second?"

Nate picked up the last of Sarah's suitcases and headed for the front door. Lauren followed with the electronic equipment he'd dismantled, leaving Sarah standing alone in the kitchen.

Sarah arranged the pictures as she wanted them. The pictures Nate had gotten from Rob's two ex-fiancées, the ones Rob had never mentioned. The one of Teddy sitting with her brother in his wheelchair, the adoring look on Teddy's face. The stills of Rob and Teddy from the surveillance feed. She left the printouts, her engagement ring, and a letter to Rob on the table, then turned and walked out without a backward glance.

III. Rob

"Sarah? Sarah, it's me. I'm home." Rob dumped his carrier and overnight bags on the floor and listened. The house was quiet. He shrugged out of his coat and opened the hall closet, freezing when he saw that it was mostly empty. Anger ignited instantly.

He dropped the coat and started toward the kitchen. Flipped on the light. At first, what he saw just looked like a couple days' worth of mail strewn across the table. Then, the pictures came into focus, and the ring, and the letter. All that hot anger turned to ice. He picked up the letter with shaking hands, tore it open, and began to read.

Rob, how could you? Was ANYTHING you ever said to me true?

Let's start with 'You were my first. My only.' Really? The two ex-fiancées told a different story. They were both very nice, btw. Pretty, too. Then there was the ring. I think that was the first time I had a hint that something wasn't quite right.

I really loved you, Rob. I did. I was over the moon when you proposed. But when you asked what kind of ring I wanted, you made fun of it. Said it was low class. I get it now. You already had a ring, left over from ex-fiancée number two. Still. Everybody has a past, Rob. I might have forgiven all that.

But I will never forgive you for what you did to Teddy. All that talk about a puppy and how much fun we'd have. You used her to isolate me. To keep me from going out and talking to people. The garbage about how she was nippy and aggressive. How I couldn't even spend time with my mom, because Teddy didn't like my brother's jerky movements or his wheelchair. That pic of Teddy with Luke tells a different story, don't you think? Then there are the pictures of you and Teddy here at home. No words needed.

This was all Teddy's doing. You have no idea. She's the one who set this all in motion and showed me the real you. She gave me a way out.

You shouldn't have picked on Teddy, Rob. Karma's a dog.

Sue Walsh is thrilled to be part of the Altitude Press anthology for a second year in a row. Sue did have a Westie as a child, and, years later, the strange encounter with the angry couple and their unfriendly dog happened almost exactly as she described it. She has thought about the oddness of that encounter many times over the years. She never saw them again or got any explanation of the event, so she decided to create "the rest of the story."

Dog Days of Summer

BY DOMINIC ANDRES

THE SUMMER SUN DOUSED the world in heat. It sank into the asphalt street, dried the grass into a brown doormat, and would have cooked an egg if anyone had asked.

Frank was not asking. It was too hot for eating, too hot for anything but an iced drink. Sweat ran down his face and soaked a damp ring into the neck of his T-shirt. A few drops escaped into space, fell for a moment, and vanished into the churned-up dirt clods below. His shovel bit into the dusty soil, scraping a few pebbles, shifting load after load to fill the hole. The hole which had been dug only the day before.

A few tears joined the drops of sweat, with no one but Frank to notice them. There were no observers, and there were not likely to be any. His house was small, his street remote, the nearby town rural, and his relatives were either dead or too young to know him. Surrounded by orange orchards and berry fields, his Southern California exile was beautiful but complete.

Frank stepped back, stabbing the shovel's blade into the pile of dirt. Searching his palm for a splinter, he cursed and wiped his eyes with his free hand, a hand as worn as old leather. He ran his fingers through graying hair. The hole was more than half-filled, no hint of yellow fur showing through. There was time before sundown for a break, so he stepped back and pulled a beer from the foam cooler lying on the wooden picnic table. His eyes wandered from his feet to the hole, then further, looking out to the brown-and-green mottled mountains on the horizon.

The beer cooled his throat, and his mind stepped away from the moment, away to when Tammy was still alive. Away to the animal shelter in town where a golden puppy had lain, looking out at him with a lolling tongue and eyes that spoke to him. *Hey old man,* they'd said, though he wasn't so old then as now. *We'd make a good pair. How 'bout it?*

Frank had agreed, and that was that.

On Wednesday morning, two days after the burial, Frank slept until after noon. No dog to feed meant no obligations meant no reason to get out of bed.

Eventually, he walked out into the hall, bare feet padding on worn carpet. His steps took him to the front door to get the daily paper. Reading was something to do, and so, every day, he learned about the goings-on in the nearby town—the local car shows, the new businesses opening and old ones closing, and generally all the same things which fill the black print of the local newspapers of dusty California townships.

His fingers closed on the knob of the front door, a door which almost glowed under a new coat of crisp, white paint that had been applied only a few weeks ago, although those weeks already felt like months. The morning brightness forced his eyes closed. When he opened them, he saw that Tammy was, as usual, waiting with the newspaper held gently in her mouth.

"Morning, girl," he said with a still slightly bleary smile.

Then he blinked. Blinked again. He closed his eyes, rubbed them. This time, when he opened them, Tammy still sat there, her tail slapping the concrete steps with a light tapping sound.

"I...What? Tammy? No, that can't be right. What a resemblance, though." He stopped speaking and examined the dog's face. He paused on the eyes. *Quite a pair we make, eh?* The same expression as in the shelter. He checked her for an old scar, for the slightly bad foot. Both were present, although there was no longer any hint of gray in her fur. He looked at the place on her torso where she'd been hit by the car. There was a scar there, too, now, in place of the fatal wound that had been there before.

His dog was back from the dead, and that last detail didn't make the slightest difference. Kneeling beside her, he cried a little, and she pushed in against his chest. He gave himself a moment, then got up and walked inside, looking back every few seconds to see that she was still following him. She was there every time.

The kitchen was old, same as the rest of the house. The faded hall carpet stopped at the door and was replaced by tile, rubbed smooth with age, cool in the shady room. Frank reached into a cabinet below the sink and pulled out her food and water bowls. They were a matched set, plain steel with rubber bases. Under the sink they had been nicely out of sight, but now they were useful once more. He filled them and, as Tammy went to eat, sat down at the kitchen table with a glass of cold milk. He sipped and enjoyed the feeling of having company again.

The next two months passed just as they had before Tammy's death. Early July turned to mid-August, the heat continued, and the papers kept coming to the door. Frank bought and sold a little produce with the nearest neighbors and went into town to see the Friday night car shows.

As for Tammy, she was in perfect health, even better than before. Soon after she'd arrived, she'd even begun to gain weight. As her midsection continued to grow, however, Frank realized that, somehow, she was pregnant.

It was strange, but there was no sense in fretting over it. She was back, and that was enough.

Then, a few days from the end of August, Tammy disappeared. Frank assumed it was just to have her puppies, and so it wasn't a shock when, one cool evening, she came trotting up the driveway. She was accompanied by two individuals. One was a single puppy trotting along beside her with the awkward gait of someone still getting used to his paws. The other was a man in a dark suit striding up the drive behind the canines. Tammy kept glancing back at him, her tongue hanging out as his carefully shined Oxfords crunched in the gravel, reflecting the setting sun like black mirrors. His suit, which had somehow remained entirely untouched by the summer dust, presented a stark contrast to his pale, almost eggshell-white skin. He would have been intimidating but for the broad smile with which he faced the world.

"Beautiful dog there, friend," he said, speaking before Frank could greet him. His voice carried an accent, but Frank couldn't place its origin.

"Thanks," Frank said. "Not many visitors out here."

"I'd imagine. Nice and remote." The man gestured to the mountains, continuing all the while towards the picnic table, until he stood only six feet away. When he stopped, Tammy stopped with him and sat down at his side.

"Just a second, sorry," Frank said to the man. "Tammy, come 'ere girl."

Tammy made no move to approach.

"Come gal, get on over," he said, frowning at her.

She looked up at the stranger, and he nodded, and then she walked over to Frank and laid her muzzle on his lap.

"That's strange," he said. "She always obeyed me before." He eyed the man's face for a reaction.

The stranger kept his smile, but it shrank and grew sad. Then he flickered, his appearance changing for the briefest of moments.

Frank's chest tightened, and his muscles tensed with a burst of adrenaline. For a moment, the world had become dark and cold, and the man standing in front of him had been paler. The flesh had disappeared from the man's face and hands, leaving them skeletal. Then the moment was gone, and everything was back the same, except that the setting sun was no longer reflected in those carefully shined shoes. Dusk had come.

"Frank, I came to let you know that I'll be taking Tammy back," the man said. "I assume you know who I am."

Frank nodded. "I know you're Death." His throat was dry, but he pushed out a few more words. "Why'd you give her back? Why, if it could only be for a few months?"

Death seemed to consider the question for several seconds. "The afterlife needs dogs, too, and nothing can be born in the Land of the Dead."

Frank thought of the Greek myths he'd read as a child, of three-headed beasts.

"Also, you always took good care of her, and you deserved a reward for that."

"She was reward enough," Frank managed to say before looking down, flushed.

Death nodded. "I'm sure she was. Still, I'd like to do something for you. Not often you get to bring someone light in my line of work, you know? That's why I brought you this fellow." Death squatted down and pushed the puppy forward, and it went trotting over towards Frank. "He wouldn't be much use for us. Wrong color, and not enough heads." The puppy panted.

"I...thank you. I don't know what to say..." Frank trailed off. *Will she be alright?* he wondered. Before he could ask, Death spoke.

"Yes, she'll be fine."

"Thanks again, then," Frank said. "Can I have a second with her?"

"Of course." Death walked a few yards back down the drive and looked out towards the mountains.

"Hey girl," Frank said, rubbing Tammy under the chin.

Her eyes looked up to him and he saw words in them once again: *We were quite a pair, but now I've brought you a new companion.*

"Thanks," he said. "Thank you, Tammy." He scratched her just behind the ear. Death was right, it was time. He could see the gray in her fur again.

She pulled her head up, turned toward Death, and walked over to him. Together, they set out down the asphalt road, following it toward the mountains until they reached a bend and were lost from sight.

Frank was left with the puppy, which started yipping at him, demanding food. He rubbed it around the ears. "Alright you," he said. "Come on over to the kitchen, then."

The pup barked and followed him inside, and they left the mountains at their backs.

Born and raised in small-town California, Dominic Andres is a recent college graduate and a writer of both fiction and nonfiction. He travels as often and reads as much as he can. His favorite drink is a Mojito.

MYTH,
FOLKLORE &
ALLEGORY

To Every Dog His Day

BY LISA TIMPF

SPRINGTIME BLOOMED IN THE world above. It had been ages since I'd walked out under the open skies, but Persephone had described the phenomenon of spring often enough that I could picture the verdant world coming back to life: The delicate scent of flowers. The return of warmth after the long winter.

Down here in the Underworld, things were different.

Water dripped ceaselessly from rock formations, the sound just far enough off-rhythm to disturb sleep. The smell of ozone wafted on the dank air. The humidity gave one's skin the sensation of being crawled upon by unwholesome insects. As if that wasn't enough, distant moans and mutters gave testimony to the sorry state of the inhabitants.

In other words, it was business as usual.

It was the very sameness, year after year, which endeared me to this place—and drove my partner Persephone back to the vibrant, living world each spring.

The Underworld may not have changed over the centuries, but that didn't mean I had to remain behind the times. I wandered into my study, with Cerberus padding at my heels, and examined the 2024 calendar on my desk. I cherished it all the more because Persephone had given it to me. "It'll help you keep track of the days until I return," she'd said.

I'd dutifully crossed off the squares marking the passage of the days after her departure at the spring equinox.

Those days seemed longer this year than they had in the past. Maybe it's because business had slowed down to a trickle. Nobody paid much attention to the ancient deities anymore. Inhabitants of the World Above seemed too busy worshipping themselves or their new gods, Social Media and Conspicuous Consumption. Even Persephone got little respect these days when she wandered the upper lands. That didn't stop her doing what she could to help humans with their agricultural efforts.

I wasn't privy to where other religions' dead went, though I'd heard rumors. As for our version of the Underworld, we hadn't seen new clients in—well, too long. Without the influx of new blood, the inhabitants of my particular Underworld had settled into a grudging acceptance of their bleak existence. Even the cries from Tartarus lacked the verve of earlier times. And Sisyphus no longer grumbled as he rolled his rock up the hill. Instead, he claimed to enjoy the workout. Just the other day, he beseeched me to admire his bulging calves and well-defined quads. I had to admit, he'd put a finely tuned Olympic athlete to shame.

Nobody had tried to escape for centuries. Though that made my job less stressful, sometimes I longed for action. I yawned and shook the hourglass to ensure the sand hadn't gotten stuck. How would I endure the hours and weeks and months until Persephone's return? I was tempted to count the days, to see how many remained, but thought better of it.

Cerberus thrust one of his three muzzles into my hand and whimpered. I patted his heads gently, giving equal time to each. The snakes wreathing his neck dangled limp as the hound tucked his reptilian tail between his legs and flattened his ears. Clearly, he missed Persephone, too.

Distant splashing caught my attention. Cerberus raised his head and flared his nostrils.

A thrill ran through me. Perhaps we had incoming clients!

I jogged to the Acheron, Cerberus at my heels. But when I arrived, my step slowed, and my shoulders slumped. I saw only Charon, poling his way across the river.

"What's going on?" I snapped the words, and the boatman turned his head slowly, his hangdog expression even sadder than usual.

Ashamed of making my faithful subordinate uncomfortable, I modified my approach. "Er—I mean—do you have some pickups to make today?"

"Nope. I'm just getting my cardio workout." Charon wheezed as his barge progressed sluggishly through the stagnant waters.

I grimaced. I wasn't sure how much of a workout his ancient heart could sustain. "Don't overdo it."

Still, I understood his motivation. Exercise was a good remedy when one felt down. I'd often found that a brisk walk with Cerberus through the lava fields cheered me up.

Maybe everyone should try it.

I tried to imagine what it might be like if all of the Underworld's denizens took turns walking Cerberus. The poor dog would be exhausted.

Fine, so that wouldn't work. But surely there must be something I could do to lighten the mood down here. Witnessing the residents' communal sadness made me miss Persephone more.

After a moment's thought, I had an idea. I could storm Up Above and demand Persephone's return. Life in the Underworld always seemed lighter with her presence. Everyone felt it. Besides, the humans didn't deserve her—just look at the terrible things they'd done to their planet.

I turned to Charon, ready to ask for a ride across the river. The request died on my lips.

I thought of how Persephone's mood lifted each year as the spring equinox approached. How she returned to the

Underworld each fall, rejuvenated by the months spent Up Above. Asking her to come back now was out of the question. She'd only resent me for it. Besides, without the opportunity to recharge her spirits in the upper world, her presence wouldn't have the usual effect.

If there was a way out of this funk, I'd have to find it without her.

Thinking about Persephone made me think of the calendar she'd given me. She'd sprung for a version that listed every "special day" celebrated by humans throughout the year. And there were a lot of special days, everything from National Kale Day and Moldy Cheese Day to Take a Hike Day and Pie in the Face Day.

Thinking of the latter, I grimaced. I'd better not let word get around down here about Pie in the Face Day. I wanted to lift the mood, but not enough to be the victim of a slapstick comedy stunt.

I shook my head. I'd lost my train of thought. There'd been something about the calendar when I'd checked it earlier this morning.

I closed my eyes, trying to remember.

Then I opened them again. April 10th was National Hug Your Dog Day. That's what I'd noticed. I'd thought to myself that I'd have to make a point of showing Cerberus some love, and then had promptly forgotten.

Until now.

Smiling, I leaned over to give Cerberus some affection, and paused.

Maybe this day could be about more than me. Maybe it could serve as a way to make the day brighter for all of us.

I decided to test my theory on Charon, who'd poled back to the shore and sat huddled on his barge, breathing heavily.

"Do you know what day it is?" I strove, with mixed results, to speak with an upbeat tone.

Charon stared at me as though I'd lost my mind.

I squared my shoulders. This was no time for doubt. "It's National Hug Your Dog Day."

"National? For what nation?"

"Does it matter?"

"I suppose not." Charon's knees creaked as he crouched down. He spread his arms in invitation. Cerberus raced toward him. To someone not familiar with Cerberus and his ways, that stampeding approach, the thundering of paws, the hissing of the now-alert snake-mane, might have been off-putting. But Charon simply absorbed the dog's leap and cuddled him.

After a few minutes, Charon looked up. "I feel better. You might be on to something."

Barely suppressing a grin, I set off to make the rounds of the Underworld. Though the inhabitants regarded Cerberus and I with suspicion as we approached, they cheered up when I suggested they show some love for everyone's favorite three-headed dog. They all took a turn massaging his ears or patting his mottled coat.

As I wandered deeper into the Underworld, I heard the rumble of a rolling boulder gathering speed as it approached the bottom of a hill. *It's just Sisyphus,* I told myself.

Sure enough, as I drew nearer, I saw Sisyphus position himself behind the wayward rock for another uphill climb.

My eyes narrowed as I approached him. He'd claimed to be taking Camus's advice and seeking meaning in the struggle rather than being put off by continual failure. But were his words genuine, or mere pretense?

I shrugged. He deserved his chance to enjoy Cerby's company just as much as anyone.

I held the rock for Sisyphus while he took a break and patted the dog. After spending a few moments thusly, Sisyphus shot me a sly glance and took a few steps away from the hill, as though to make an escape.

I felt a moment's despair, followed by chagrin. What would Persephone say if she could see me now?

But I should have known better than to doubt Cerberus. The dog had enjoyed the attention, but he knew his duty. Cerby moved to face Sisyphus, baring his teeth.

One head would be bad enough, but three, plus the extended snake-mane—let's just say Sisyphus seemed only too happy to resume his position before matters went from bad to worse. "Focus on the journey, not the destination," he mumbled as he once again began to roll the rock uphill.

As I wandered back to my abode at the end of the long day, I thought about the calendar Persephone had left me. Perhaps she'd hoped I'd learn the truth for myself—that our lives are enriched not by counting down to some anticipated event, but by valuing each day for what it offers.

I knew I'd still miss Persephone in the months to come. But I also realized that would make our autumn reunion all the sweeter. Besides, I had my three-headed hound to keep me company. What more could I ask?

I patted Cerby's nearest noggin. "Should we do this again tomorrow?"

I interpreted the deep, three-toned woof as a gesture of assent.

"Very well. I'll mark it on the calendar."

Retired HR and communications professional Lisa Timpf lives in Simcoe, Ontario, Canada. Her stories have appeared in New Myths, Cosmic Crime, Home for the Howlidays, *and other venues. Lisa's haibun collection,* In Days to Come, *is available from Hiraeth Publishing. You can find out more about Lisa's writing at LisaTimpf.blogspot.com*

The Other Minmose

BY ANGELA M MCCANN

MINMOSE'S FACE WAS STILL.

Pepy cocked his head, wagging his tail and giving a few quick barks as if that might make the silent figure smile. Or open his mouth. Or acknowledge him in any way. The dog hadn't heard his own name in all the time he'd sat alone in this stone room, with nobody but this still, staring figure for company. He was beginning to fear that Minmose had forgotten who he was.

Not that this one had ever spoken, but there was time yet.

With a desolate whine, his dark eyes flickered to the walls surrounding them. People had spent many hours covering the walls in little shapes, which they seemed to understand, though Pepy could not make any sense of them. A few images were familiar. He barked happily at pictures of his fellow dogs and wagged his tail at the sight of each person, while giving every cat image he spotted a well-deserved growl.

None of them talked to him.

They were silent, just like this Minmose.

The other Minmose, *his* Minmose, did talk.

He also threw sticks and gave Pepy belly rubs every day.

Pepy missed that Minmose, the one who often walked around the sandy dunes as other men loudly made shapes out of stone. There were many rooms like this one, all of them covered in those funny shapes. Minmose would look at them all, giving commands and praise to every person he passed, with Pepy close by his side.

He'd told the dog that these rooms were places of rest, and that Pepy's job was guarding the rooms and the workers who made them. Because he had spent nearly his whole life at Minmose's side, Pepy took great pride in this role. And he did his job with vigor. He got rid of snakes who may hurt his people, he warned other dogs to keep their distance, and he chased away bad men trying to steal whatever they could.

He didn't chase cats though, not after getting told off for cornering a little grey one. Minmose said she was special and that she was beloved by Bastet. Pepy didn't know who Bastet was but considered her very silly for loving such a tricky beast; she would be far better giving her love to a loyal dog. And the cat, later named Henut and given a collar like him, seemed not to do any work other than chasing the odd mouse or scorpion, a task Pepy could have managed with ease. She was lazy and often teased him, but he was a good dog and so did as he was told and left her alone.

Minmose said Pepy was beloved as well, by someone called Anubis. He'd shown the dog a picture of this Anubis, who had a head like Pepy's and a body like Minmose's. The figure had confused him at first, but now he considered their combined shapes to be a symbol of the friendship and undying bond between dog and man. This pleased him greatly and made him feel proud to be beloved by such a being.

There was a picture of Anubis depicted close to where this Minmose sat still, and Pepy stood up on his hind legs to give him an affectionate lick.

Then his ears pricked up at the sudden sound of a distant bark.

It sounded like Kanefru, a pretty dog who helped him guard the rooms in the sand alongside the old dog Ramose and their newest addition, Nakht, who was barely out of puppyhood. Pepy had been trying to teach the excitable youth to be strong and controlled, but Nakht often talked too much. And there was his yapping reply to Kanefru now, soon echoed by the gruffer bark of Ramose.

Normally, Pepy would add his own bark to the chorus, but tonight he felt like being alone. Besides, he wasn't sure if they would expect him there. He'd been kept away from the stone rooms for a while since his Minmose disappeared. Not imprisoned by any means, he was being well looked after by his master's wife Nefty. She was nice. She fed him tasty meat and always petted his head.

But she wasn't Minmose.

Pepy had to stay with Minmose.

And Minmose was here.

That's what his Minmose had said when he'd shown Pepy this still version. He'd said that when he was gone from this world his *Ka* would inhabit this version, and he could always be found here. Pepy didn't understand what a *Ka* was, but the way Minmose talked about it meant it was important. Food had been put here, so the *Ka* needed to eat, and as the rooms had been called a place of rest, it clearly needed to sleep.

He was starting to wonder if this *Ka* was doing everything Minmose had been struggling with. Pepy had watched his master move slower and struggle to get out of bed, growing wrinkled and thin despite keeping his smile. A man had come with funny smelling, sticky stuff, but that didn't help. Then, one day, several men had taken Minmose away, carrying him into a dark room that Pepy was forbidden to enter.

Minmose didn't come out of that room, and Nefty had started telling Pepy to stay home with her. She seemed sad. He wanted to cheer her up, but by then he'd realized that Minmose had clearly come here like he said he would. His *Ka* was here, and because Pepy had sworn to stay by his master's side, he had snuck out of the house to come and be with him.

315

And now he was here, with this other Minmose that didn't move or talk to him.

A low whine left Pepy's throat...then a smell caught his attention.

Men.

Unknown men.

Bad men.

Their voices, hushed and sharp, soon reached his ears. This wasn't the first time he'd had to deal with intruders, but their arrival felt even more enraging now. He wanted to be with Minmose, and these men were here to ruin his work. The whine transitioned to a growl, his fur standing on end as the voices grew closer and closer. It was strange that the others had not yet barked, but no matter.

However they got past the other dogs, this would be as far as they came.

With a final glance at the still Minmose, Pepy slunk out of the room, keeping his body low to remain out of sight of the intruders. It was dark outside, but the moon illuminated the sandy dunes. Pepy paused just at the entrance, his gaze flickering this way and that until there they were, a pair of bald heads crouched low and turned away but moving in his direction.

He took the opportunity to scramble up to the roof of Minmose's room, lying flat and watching their approach. He caught sight of tools in their hands, tools similar to what the workers used to make the rooms and shapes on the walls, as they hissed to each other like cobras.

"...avoided those mutts..."

"...be quick..."

"...rich man recently died..."

The voices were getting louder, and they were coming straight towards Minmose's room.

Pepy stood up to his full height and gave a single, sharp, resounding bark.

The two men jerked to a stop, one dropping a tool onto the sand as their heads tilted back to make out Pepy towering above them. The moon shone directly behind the dog, casting his growing shadow so that it covered the two with his immense form. He could smell their fear, could see their eyes widen as they realised their mistake.

He was Pepy—beloved of Anubis, protector of these rooms, and friend of Minmose.

These bad men would not get away.

He growled and barked again, exposing his fangs as his shoulders moved up and down, preparing to pounce. One of the men shouted at him and threw a tool. It fell short of striking Pepy, but the force with which it had been thrown knocked a chunk from the corner of the roof.

Minmose's roof.

Pepy looked from the damage to the man...and then leapt.

His weight knocked the intruder to the ground, while his fangs quickly found purchase in the flesh of the neck. The man flailed and screamed, trying to get the dog off him, but Pepy held on, determined to repay the damage done to Minmose's room.

The man's companion yelled in shock and turned to leave, but his cries were quickly echoed by the furious barking of Kanefru, Ramose, and Nakht, who soon appeared at the room's entrance.

A moment later, the young dog lunged at the second man's feet to knock him off balance while the other two snapped at his limbs. He was quickly on the ground, scrambling away on all fours and rolling out of sight as Nakht and Ramose chased after him.

Kanefru barked a few more times before stopping her pursuit and turning to look at Pepy, who raised his dripping maw from the neck of the intruder. The man was still now; he wouldn't be able to cause any further damage here.

The two dogs approached each other, exchanging sniffs, licks, and comforting nuzzles. It lasted longer than it normally did after an enemy had been vanquished. Pepy cocked his head as Kanefru leaned her head against his neck. She seemed to have missed him, or perhaps she knew he was missing his Minmose and was simply offering some affection to make him feel better. Despite his desire to be alone with the other Minmose, he could not deny he felt happy to spend time with her again. To show this, he leaned against her, too.

Nakht's excited barking broke the two apart; it seemed the other man had also been dealt with. Kanefru made to follow the sound, then hesitated, looking back to give Pepy a small *yip*.

He let out a *ruff* in return, nudging her tail to encourage her to go ahead.

After a few more false starts, she finally disappeared over the moonlit sand.

He stared after her for a while and then returned to the stone room.

Soon, he was standing in front of the other Minmose, licking his maw clean as he looked up at the still face. He had done his job by protecting this room from those bad men, just as he had done for years by Minmose's side. Normally, this would be where his master petted his head and told him he was a good boy.

Watching the still face silently for a few more minutes, Pepy eventually padded over and licked one of the unmoving hands resting on Minmose's lap. It was cold and had the same taste as the wall, but he still rested his head on top of it and settled in for the night.

This wasn't *his* Minmose, but it was still Minmose. And as long as he was here, Pepy would stay here too.

Angela M McCann is a British author currently living in Liverpool, having moved there to get her university degree in Egyptology. Horror is the main genre of fiction she likes to write, but she also dabbles in fantasy, sci-fi, and historical fiction. When not writing, she enjoys gaming, sewing, and baking.

The Beast of Burnell

BY GEMMA CHURCH

JANE'S FATHER NEVER HAD time to read her a bedtime story. There was too much to do in the evening:
scrubbing the blood from the countertops, floors, and
cutting boards; restocking the shelves with sundries;
and hauling hunks of meat to the cool cellar to keep
them from spoiling.

Every night, Jane would push her little barrow through
Burnell's streets to dispose of the shop's waste outside
the city walls. It was always a long walk. The barrow
was heavy, but Jane was a strong and straight-backed

twelve-year-old, marching over the cobbles and ignoring the jeers from the shopboys slumped in their doorways.

Jane told herself that she cared neither about their taunts nor her lack of a bedtime story as she curled up under the covers, listening to the *swish-swish* of her father sharpening his knives and cleavers in the next room.

As she slept, Jane dreamt only of one thing: the city library. Though she passed it every evening, she could not leave the full barrow on the streets, and it was always shut when she returned.

The library was a wonder. It was a round building, large and ivy-cloaked with a variety of marble figurines poking their heads out from the thick curtain of pointed leaves. The effigies were similar to the grotesques found on most gothic structures. But, compared to those rough and twisted depictions, the library's carvings were detailed and incredibly lifelike, painted to give clear representations of people and creatures both real and imagined. There were hundreds of these figureheads, maybe thousands, a stony crowd as plentiful and diverse as the stars in the night sky. Some of the figures looked down to the ground, others turned to face one another, heads bent in conversation, but most gazed at the heavens. Jane had memorized each one as she passed with her barrow.

Every night, she dreamed of stepping inside and navigating the library's towering shelves, her fingertips skimming the leather-bound tomes as the musty smell of paper and ink cocooned her. But the scenes were only snatches of her imagination, since she had never actually set foot inside the library. In fact, she had only ever touched one book in her entire life.

Every morning, she would wake to find a steaming mug of tea on her bedside table, her father sitting next to her bed with his apron already on, and said book resting in his lap. It was bound in weathered leather with pages yellowed with age and edges softened from countless readings.

"How about a story to start the day?" he'd ask her.

Jane looked forward to this question each morning. Her favorite story, the one she got him to repeat until his voice nearly ran dry, was "The Beast of Burnell."

"Why do you want to hear that one all the time?" he would mock-complain as Jane asked him to tell it again. "Would you not prefer some tale about brave knights saving pretty princesses?"

To this, Jane would pull a face and pretend to be sick. And her father would tell her the tale about the bloodthirsty hound with its sharp fangs that prowled in the shadows. The story always seemed so harmless in the day's new light.

But one evening, as Jane left the city walls with her barrow and the echoes of the boys' heckles rattling around her head, the story reignited in her mind, causing her strong arms to tremble. Barely taking the time to observe the library, she glanced at the shadows, expecting The Beast of Burnell to jump out and attack at any moment.

"It's just a story. Words cannot hurt you," she mumbled repeatedly under her breath.

It had been a long day; her feet stung, and her back ached. She was later than usual, and the darkness was seeping in. Jane quickened her pace as the unmistakable odor of the city dump hit the back of her throat.

The barrow's wheel squeaked in rhythm to her mantra.

"It's just a story. Words cannot hurt you. It just a—"

Jane froze. Rising from the heap of rubbish, a black shape eclipsed the slant sun on the horizon. It was the unmistakable shape of a dog.

Her mouth turned to dust, and her arms faltered. The barrow tipped over as bones, fat, and offal slopped onto the ground.

The dog advanced.

He was huge and black, and he bounded toward Jane with a lolloping gait. A loop of white neck hair stood out against the black as his pointed teeth flashed against the darkness, sharp as her father's knives.

Jane fell to the ground and curled into a ball, hiding behind the upturned barrow. Cold blood seeped into her hair, but she did not move as The Beast of Burnell towered over her, panting. She caught the scent of his warm breath. It smelt of...roasted ham...with a slight undercurrent of stale ginger nut biscuits, not the metallic smell of death she expected.

Then, something even more unexpected happened: The Beast licked her head. Twice. His tongue was the size of a dinner plate, and it left her covered in drool.

"Ugh!" she shouted.

The Beast of Burnell stepped back and barked in a manner that almost sounded like laughter. Then, shockingly, he spoke. "Are you alright, little one? I apologize. The smell of the meat does tend to make me drool more than usual. May I?"

Mute, Jane nodded. She watched as the dog began to wolf down the contents of her upturned barrow. "A-Are you not going to eat me?" she finally asked him.

The dog looked up from his food and laughed his woofing laugh once more. "Eat you? Why no, little one, you're the person who feeds me every night with these scraps. That would be most illogical."

"But you're The Beast of Burnell," Jane whispered.

"Oh, yes. I forgot about that tale. Is it still going around the city?"

Jane nodded again. "Well, me and Dad still read it. It's the only book we have. It's old. I don't think any-one else reads it or remembers it."

"You own one book? Is the city library closed?"

"No. But it's always shut whenever I pass it. And I never have time to visit when it's open on account of all the work in Dad's shop."

The dog nodded and, having finished the scraps, licked his lips.

"So, you're not going to eat me?"

"Oh no. Contrary to the rumors of sugar and spice, little girls are actually rather gristly," he said with a wink.

"And you didn't murder and eat The Bishop of Burnell?"

The dog raised a hairy eyebrow. "That bishop was a greedy old man. Did you know he carried at least two pork pies in each pocket of his vestments, everywhere he went? Gobbling them down after he visited the starved souls in the city's workhouse? He died of a heart attack. I saw it happen, and I was merely hungry. People drew the wrong conclusions when they found me bent over his body with pie innards all over my nose. And after the way they tried to hunt me down, pitchforks piercing the sky, well. I decided to retreat to outside the city walls. This is where I've stayed, making the surrounding forests my home. I only come here to eat whatever you and the other shop girls throw away."

"That explains the ham and biscuits on your breath earlier," Jane said. "But couldn't you come back to the city and just tell people you weren't what they thought? Or find your own home?"

"A naïve assumption. Were you not listening to the story? When I lived in the city, no one was willing to give me a chance because they didn't like the look of me. They were blind and deaf to my suffering because I was deemed too big and scary." Here, the dog nodded sagely, as if he was The Bishop of Burnell standing at the pulpit and not a stray at the city's dumping grounds. "Likewise, you must listen more carefully to the stories you're told, little one. You must question everything."

Jane frowned, saddened by both the story and her short-sightedness. "I'm sorry."

"What for?"

"For believing the story about you. Maybe I could try to sneak out something better than this spoiled meat, to make up for things. We often have leftover pork pies."

Drool cascaded from the dog's mouth as he howled up at the moon with joy. "Oh! Could you? I would forever be in your debt."

"My debt?"

He bowed until the tip of his nose touched her boot. "Yes. I will not accept charity. So, ask what you will of me, and I will gratefully abide in exchange for a pork pie."

Jane opened her mouth and then stopped. The first thought that flashed through her mind was to set the dog on the boys who teased her every evening. But then she realized that would damage the dog's reputation further. More importantly, she didn't really care what insults those dimwits fired at her; there were more important words in the world than theirs. "I think I have a solution to all our problems," she said finally, unwrapping her scarf and using it to form a loose harness around the dog. She tied the ends to the barrow's handles.

Every evening henceforth, the dog (who Jane later found out was called Bernard and not The Beast of Burnell) trotted through the city to the butcher's shop. Occasionally, he would flash his fangs at the shopboys and quietly delight when they squealed and ran inside.

Once Bernard reached the butcher's shop, Jane would hitch him to the barrow using the makeshift harness her father had fashioned out of leather scraps. Together, they would walk through the city to the library, where they would part ways. Bernard would dutifully take the barrow to the dumping grounds and back while Jane would feed her mind with all the words the world had to offer.

When Bernard returned the barrow to the shop, Jane and her father would give him as many pork pies as he wanted. They offered him shelter and a home as well, but

Bernard always refused, claiming he preferred the solitude of the world outside the city walls.

When winter crept in, however, Bernard would occasionally snooze by the hearth as Jane read by the light of the fire. Those naps soon grew into deep sleeps until it was generally agreed that it would be far more logical for Bernard to stay with Jane and her father permanently.

Bernard insisted on earning his keep, which was fortuitous as there was still much to do in the evenings. He helped in every way he could, with only two demands: a full belly and a bedtime story read to him every night by Jane.

In this manner, the years passed. Jane and Bernard's hair greyed, and their bodies began to fail them. But their minds stayed as sharp as her father's blades.

One evening, Jane appeared not with a book in her hands but a sheet of paper. The ink was still wet; it glistened in the firelight and stained her fingertips as she read the words aloud.

Lying down and closing his eyes for the last time, Bernard thought the story—about a dog once known as The Beast who found his home in a city called Burnell—was the best one he'd ever heard.

With two degrees in physics, Gemma Church has worked in science communication for twenty-plus years. She has an Undergraduate Diploma in Creative Writing from Cambridge University, and her short stories appear in numerous publications. She also has a small, very un-beastlike dog called Newton who is always the first to hear any story she writes and who inspired this one.

Warp and Woof

BY LAURIE HERLICH

THE GREAT HUNTER AND I loved to play fetch. Orion captured stray asteroids or comets and attached them to his arrows. Then, he nocked each arrow on the string, drew and anchored the bow, took aim, and *twang!*

I chased the projectiles as they flew through the galaxy while avoiding burning stars and dodging moons and planets. I held my ears close to my head, tongue lolling, feeling the space dust flow through my fur. Asteroids seemed gritty to my fangs, but comets buzzed pleasantly on my tongue. They tasted sort of spicy, actually. As far as I was concerned, Orion and I could continue this game for all eternity.

Meanwhile, Loki escaped his bonds and wandered the Milky Way, looking for mischief to stir up. Thor had blocked him from Midgard, and Odin forbade him to enter Asgard. He could not take direct revenge against his wife, Sigyn, who had unintentionally dripped snake venom on his skin, causing him to writhe in pain. The heat of summer increased Loki's restlessness. On whom else could he exact vengeance? Where else could he wreak havoc? What else could he entwist?

He espied Side as she was weaving clothes for her daughters. Loki cast a spell, so the warp and woof knotted up and twisted. Side removed the fibers from the loom and reattached them, but, mysteriously, the shuttle became entangled once more.

The naughty deity shook with laughter, which led to Side's young daughters grabbing the loose ends of the threads and running through the dwelling. She chased them until her foot caught on a strand of floss, causing her to trip. Side rolled over, stood up, and called for her daughters to obey. Still enchanted, they giggled and refused, so Side stomped her foot and wiped the perspiration from her brow.

"Orion," she sang. "My love, come to me."

As her melodious voice rang out among the stars, my ears perked up. Glancing at Orion, I pointed my nose in Side's direction.

"Thank you, faithful friend, for alerting me," he said in response. "Come along."

I followed Orion, wagging my tail and panting happily. The two of us surfed the Milky Way until we reached his wife's dwelling.

Upon entering, we saw Side sobbing with her face in her hands. Orion knelt by her chair and brushed the hair from her eyes. "You've called me, and here I am. How may I serve?" he asked as I licked my mistress's hand to comfort her.

Side put her arms around her husband. "Please help me, Orion, I am so frustrated. The fibers are knotted, tangled, and strewn about the dwelling. They will make uncomfortable clothes for our little daughters. It is as though my loom has been enchanted. I need the cocoons of silkworms to weave soft dresses. I hear the Seven Sisters have a great many."

Orion kissed her gently before giving his beard a thoughtful stroke. "I can't help thinking some mischief is afoot," he said. "The only thing you've ever twisted is when you wove our hearts so wonderfully together. Nonetheless, you wish for silk from the Pleiades, and you shall have it."

Their daughters giggled from the other side of a drapery, making my ears twitch. I corralled them for Orion, who scooped them up in his strong arms. "Time for a nap, little ones," he announced, carrying the protesting toddlers to their beds.

When they were gone, I sighed softly, nuzzling Side to comfort her.

In return, she stroked my head. "Thank you, dear Sirius. I know you'll always be my husband's faithful companion. Oh, your ears are so heavenly soft." She bent to whisper in them, "Keep him safe, please."

I wagged my tail, so Side would understand I would do whatever was necessary to keep my promise to her.

Orion returned and slung his bow and quiver of arrows over his shoulder. "Come, Sirius," he commanded. "We have a mission." He strode purposefully from the dwelling, and I eagerly followed in his wake.

We sailed through the Milky Way, searching for the Seven Sisters. Loki placed five red herrings in our way, but I sniffed them out and alerted Orion to the deception.

I caught the scent of Hermod the Swift. He knew where the ladies were hiding from Loki's mischief, but he had a warning for us: "Rumor has it the imp is making trouble for all the deity kingdoms."

I growled at the thought.

Continuing on our journey, we next encountered Taurus. Loki had provoked and teased the giant bull into a rage, causing him to snort while pawing many stars out of their positions with his hooves. One glance at Orion and the beast saw red. He blocked the path of my mighty hunter.

I tried to point Orion to an alternate route, but Taurus put his head down and charged my master, attempting to impale him with his horns.

In response, Orion removed his cloak and swung it at the bull, seeking to confuse him. They traded positions several times, and each pass only increased the bull's fury. Taurus, failing to gore the great hunter, collided with him instead. We were knocked further off course, which delayed us on our errand for Side.

Blood flowed heatedly through my body as a snarl escaped my lips. I leapt at the bull, biting him on the haunch and nipping at his hooves. Taurus turned to spear me with his horns, and we took turns charging each other.

Orion returned to the battle. He tied a golden cord behind the fletching of his arrow and took aim at Zoozve. The bolt connected, and he reeled the satellite in, telling it, "You may be small, my friend, but you are not insignificant." Then the hunter gave a mighty toss and hit Taurus in the head. "Bull's Eye," gloated my master.

Taurus was stunned long enough for us to find and visit the Pleiades.

Orion entered their workshop and bowed deeply from the waist. "Dear ladies, you know my lovely wife. There is mischief afoot, which ruined all the fibers she had. We request new supplies for her weaving."

After conferring amongst themselves, the Seven Sisters replied, "We have long been friends with Side, and so we will gift you with silk cocoons for your wife. It is Loki's misdoings at work, and we want your little daughters to have soft and lovely dresses."

Orion bowed once more. "We thank you, gracious ladies."

I wagged my tail in agreement as they packed a parcel for us to bring home. Orion placed the package of cocoons in a leather pouch tied about his waist.

We passed by Taurus on our return trip. The fierce bull awoke and charged Orion once again. Hot with anger, I felt my hackles rise, and I snarled in warning. As Taurus pawed more stars out of the way, I lunged at him, sinking my teeth into his neck. That brought the bull back to his senses, and he soon resumed guarding the Pleiades from Loki, as they hid behind his shoulder.

Whew! That was close. I retrieved Zoozve and brought the satellite to Orion, who placed his fists on his hips.

"When next I see Hermod," he announced, "I will send a message to Odin. Loki must be held responsible for his misdeeds. In the meantime, Zoozve, for your help I will place you by the side of beautiful Venus." Turning to me, he said, "Now, Sirius, let's bring our treasures back to Side. You have a great heart, my friend, and shall forevermore be with me. When summer peaks, you'll glow as the brightest star in the heavens."

Truth be told, I could already feel my joy shining from the inside out!

Laurie Herlich loves living in rural northeast Tennessee, where Story is everything. She writes flash fiction and cozy mysteries in a converted garden hut situated in her backyard. Laurie is a regular contributor to ChristianDevotions. us and won a Selah award in the Online Devotion category as well as first place two years in a row for her unpublished novella and the sequel in the Foundation Awards. She is also a contributor/performer for Jonesborough, Tennessee's StoryTown *NPR Radio Show/Podcast and is a StoryTeller with the Jonesborough Storytelling Guild.*

Printed in Great Britain
by Amazon

50519915R00199